Larissa Behrendt is Professor of Law and Director of the Jumbunna Indigenous House of Learning at the University of Technology, Sydney. She is a member of the Eualeyai/Kamilaroi nations of north-west New South Wales. Her first novel, *Home*, was the winner of the David Unaipon Award for Indigenous Writers and the Commonwealth Writers' Prize for Best First Book (South-East Asia/Pacific region).

Legacy

LARISSA BEHRENDT

UQP

First published 2009 by University of Queensland Press
PO Box 6042, St Lucia, Queensland 4067 Australia

www.uqp.com.au

Typeset in Bembo 11.5/15.5pt by Post Pre-press Group, Brisbane
Printed in Australia by McPherson's Printing Group

This project has been assisted by
the Commonwealth Government
through the Australia Council,
its arts funding and advisory body.

Cataloguing-in-Publication Data
National Library of Australia

Larissa Behrendt.
Legacy.

ISBN 978 0 7022 3733 1

1. Aboriginal Australians – Fiction. I. Title.

To my father,
Paul Behrendt,
Whom I love.
And whom I miss.
Every day.

CANBERRA, AUSTRALIA, 1972

We put the women at the front line. We thought that the police would not arrest them. Some of us were not so sure, but it was the women who insisted upon it. We had argued about it through the night and by three in the morning, they had persuaded us.

We linked arms – Aborigines and students, black and white, men and women – and surrounded the tent that had our flags flying.

We shouted, 'Land Rights Now. Land Rights Now'.

We sang 'We Shall Not Be Moved'.

Hundreds of onlookers – tourists with their cameras, public servants in their pin-striped suits – stood by and watched.

There were about sixty of us and just as many coppers. It was after ten thirty that the police started to move on us. They hit us with fists, putting four of us in the hospital. The newspaper reported that three coppers had to have x-rays.

They moved on us again three days later when we tried to rebuild our Embassy. In the morning about a hundred of us marched from the university to Parliament House. We sat down on the road and listened to speeches. About fifty coppers were watching us. We then tried to erect another tent and we formed a human shield around it. By this time there were about two hundred of us and two hundred and fifty of them. There were more arrests.

The cameras were there and we made news around the world.

A week later we had a peaceful protest and re-established our Embassy.

Above our tents we flew a flag – black for the colour of the people, red for the land and the blood that has been spilt upon it, and yellow for the sun that with its rising brings together the people and the land, always.

There was momentum. We knew that what we were fighting for was right and that we were a part of something that would have a lasting impact.

Even though I couldn't know that one day I would talk about the Tent Embassy with my daughter, tell her what happened and what we hoped for, I knew that I was making history.

Thirty Years Later . . .

PART I

I

BOSTON, UNITED STATES

Hedonophobia is the fear of pleasure. Acarophobia is the fear of itching or of the insects that cause it. Lallophobia describes the fear of speaking. If there's a name for these phobias, somewhere in the lexicon there must be a word for the fear of meetings with a doctoral supervisor. The closest word I have found is 'rhabdophobia', the fear of being punished or severely criticised.

I have a restless sleep the night before my monthly meeting with Professor Young – the third Thursday of the month. I lie awake and I think through all the questions he will ask me, anticipate his comments and criticisms of my arguments and, to the blue-grey of my streetlamp-lit room, I rehearse my answers. As I say them out loud, I sound confident. I can hear Professor Young saying, 'Yes, Simone. I had not quite thought about it that way.' And he has a look of beneficence, the same look my father would wear when I brought my school report card home or asked him questions about history or politics as he cooked in the kitchen.

The day seems long as I count down the hours to my meeting at 4 pm. I tidy the kitchen nook and then watch some television before I try to settle in to work. I attempt to read but my concentration is poor. I find myself re-reading the same passage several times, easily distracted by other thoughts – what will Professor Young ask me about? how will I answer? – and in the end I decide to pack my books and head to the café.

Many people would find the noise of a coffee shop an unproductive environment for work or study. I like being surrounded by the bustle. I try to read again but the questions in my head seem louder than the chatter around me. I open my notebook and write out some notes, the evolving structure of the whole of my thesis, just in dot points. This exercise helps me to feel in control of this overwhelming project. I find it comforting.

It is cold now but this is my second fall in Boston and I've gotten used to it. The trick to keeping warm is layering – underwear, pantyhose, jeans, socks, boots, t-shirt, sweater, coat, scarf, hat, gloves and earmuffs. When I first moved here, the summer heat was the same sticky humid kind that I was used to in Sydney – the kind that reminds you you're living near a vast body of water even if you can't see it. And then the leaves changed, crunching like fortune cookies under my boots. Soon enough it will be winter and I will be trudging through the snow.

They made a fuss of me when I arrived here though I suspected they were a little disappointed that the Aborigine who had come all the way from Australia was not darker and couldn't play the didgeridoo. 'Only men are supposed to play it,' I sniffed indignantly. But eventually I found my own rhythm in this place where I could disappear among everyone else. Where I wasn't simply 'Tony Harlowe's daughter'.

I liked Professor Young from the first time I took his class – Legal Theory in Modern Society. He was sitting in the classroom before the students arrived. Most Harvard professors wait until everyone is seated so that they can make a grand entrance. Not Professor Young. He sat at the desk at the front of the room furiously writing notes on a small piece of paper that he then folded and placed in his shirt pocket. After watching the clock tick on to five past four he stood up, and without once looking at the piece of paper he had tucked tightly away, lectured for two hours. He was the kind of man who is youthfully handsome but whose greying hair makes him look more distinguished. By the time I had written SIMONE HARLOWE on the attendance sheet, I knew I was infatuated.

The first time I opened the door to his office I had wondered how a mind that possessed the clarity of Professor Young's – a mind that could weave an argument seamlessly for two hours without prompting or diversion – could thrive in an environment of such chaos. Untidy piles of papers were strewn across the opulent oak. The walls were lined with bookshelves; paperbacks and leather-bound texts were pressed together, often doubled up on the shelves, their musty, rotting smell scenting the air. Between the worn leather chair and the large window that cast afternoon light behind him, the grey-flecked carpet was littered with overstuffed manila folders and photocopied pages, piles of seemingly neglected ideas.

'How do you find anything in here?' I asked in an attempt to sound less nervous.

'Would you believe me if I told you that I know where everything is?' Professor Young answered in his deep-toned voice. He laid his hands across the thick timber of the desk top, spreading his fingers like a duck's webbed feet. His charcoal eyes gleamed.

'No,' I smiled.

That day I had sat awkwardly in the same chair that now I so casually sling my handbag over and arrange myself in. Back then I stammered through my self-introduction and the outline of my proposed research topic, my hands sweating and twisting. Today I am more able to ease into conversation – but not completely.

When I graduated with my law degree I had worked for a while at the Legal Aid Commission – mostly family law and social security appeals – and once absorbed in the day-to-day paperwork and local court appearances of legal practice, I had longed to work on the ideas that underpin law reform. So I began to think about returning to university and doing post-graduate studies.

When I first told my father about being accepted onto the doctoral program, his palpable, unashamed excitement increased my pride. After his initial euphoria had waned a little he wanted to know more about Professor Young. 'What does he know about Aboriginal issues, about our history and culture?' He had asked the same things of all of my school teachers.

'Not much,' I had replied, ready to defend Professor Young but also to appease my father. 'Dad, I couldn't learn more about that side of it than I have from you. But Professor Young will be able to give me something different. He understands a way of thinking beyond the black letters of the law, like the links between "law" and "justice", and the power imbalance. The situation of Aboriginal people in Australia is an interesting example of the kind of things he writes about.'

This had been enough consolation for Dad, especially when weighed against the prestige of the school. And it had been a pretty accurate guess at what I would learn from Professor Young. He had taught me how to relate the abstracts of legal arguments back to the practical impacts of law. He had drummed into me how it was important to not just argue for law reform but show why it is important by looking at its impact on people's lives.

After an exchange of pleasantries, Professor Young starts the meeting with the same question as always: 'So, Simone, what is your central argument?'

It's all there in the brief I prepared for him that was delivered to his secretary on the Monday before the meeting but he makes me say it as well.

Today I shift in my seat to get comfortable, take a deep breath. 'The doctrine of discovery was a key part of international law at the time that the British claimed Australia. International law allowed for the claiming of territory if it was empty of people or had no sovereign. This was used as a justification for the settlement of Australia, even though there were clearly Aboriginal people living there who had systems of governance and sets of laws.'

'So your argument is that Aboriginal people were sovereign at the time that the British claimed Australia,' Professor Young observes.

I nod and continue. 'They did. Despite the evidence that Aboriginal people clearly had a system of laws and governance, the legal fiction of *terra nullius* eventually became part of Australian law.'

'So the whole legal system had been predicated on it,' Professor Young is looking intently at my paper. His focus is reassuring.

'That's right. And the doctrine continued until the *Mabo* case in 1992 when the High Court overturned it. But they didn't make any determination on the issue of Aboriginal sovereignty other than to say that the question of whether Australia was lawfully acquired by the British was a matter to be decided by international law, not Australian courts.'

'So they left the matter undecided?'

'Well, I argue that they replaced the legal fiction of *terra nullius* with a legal fiction of "settlement". But on the facts, Australia was conquered, not settled.'

'And if that is the case, what are the legal implications of Australia being "conquered" rather than "settled"?'

'Well, that would mean that the laws of Aboriginal people, including land ownership, should have been recognised. Recognition that Australia was conquered could give rise to the recognition of Aboriginal customs and property interests. It would give Aboriginal people leverage in asserting their rights in modern Australian society.'

Professor Young places my written brief on the desk in front of him and turns his attention to me. 'A very pretty legal argument, Simone.' He swivels his chair sideways so he can look at me but also out the window behind him when he chooses to. 'But what do you think the chances of getting this recognition of "conquest" rather than "settlement" are in practical terms? Isn't the more important question the extent to which sovereignty remains today? No matter how strong their claims to sovereignty were at the time of invasion, could Aboriginal people still meet the criteria of a sovereign nation now? Could they show things such as a defined territory, a government structure and the capacity to enter into relations with other states?'

I think about the many times I've heard my father stand to speak about all this – community forums, Land Council meetings, rallies. Since before I could walk, I had been hearing it. 'This is our land,' he'd say. 'We never gave our consent for these whitefellas to take our land, to take our children and make paternalistic laws for us. We need to make decisions ourselves, exercise our sovereignty as the Aboriginal nations of this land.'

With a lifetime of Dad's words echoing in my ears I answer Professor Young. 'I don't think Aboriginal people want to be a separate country. When we talk about "sovereignty", we are seeking recognition of our ability to speak as a nation of peoples and for recognition of our laws in Australia.'

Professor Young asks if by the term 'sovereignty' I mean the way it is understood under international law.

'Well, yes and no.' I have to think before I go further because my answer was intuitive. When Dad would talk about the "Aboriginal nation" and "Aboriginal sovereignty", he would mean the ability to make decisions for ourselves or the recognition of customary laws. But sovereignty under international law also gives the ability to make laws, impose taxes, to make war and peace and make treaties with other nations. Dad would talk of making a treaty with the Australian state and collecting a percentage of the land tax but not about having our own currency and stamps. And there is also the aspect of having territorial integrity and in all the years I've heard his speeches – the speeches of Tony Harlowe – I've never heard him mention a separate Aboriginal country. Professor Young stares out his window. The lowering sun is streaming light across his face and on to his desk. He squints slightly. 'I don't think so,' I say to him finally.

'I think you're approaching the question the wrong way around.' He picks up my brief and looks at the front page. 'Your question, Simone, as you've told me at almost every meeting we've had is "how do we recognise Aboriginal sovereignty in Australia?" And in asking that question you are defining sovereignty by using international law but the more interesting approach to the question is to define "sovereignty" in the way that Aboriginal people would.'

He is right. And I see it clearly as soon as he says it. It's so obvious but it has taken this white man in Boston to make me see that I've not been asking the question from an Aboriginal point of view. How could this happen to the daughter of Tony Harlowe who had heard nothing but the Aboriginal point of view all her life?

Have I become so captured by legal arguments that I've forgotten why I began studying law in the first place?

Professor Young saves me from having to speak. 'Well, perhaps that's the issue we should focus on at our next meeting.' He places my brief into a tray marked 'Filing'. 'Develop that idea further,' he adds. 'What is it that Aboriginal people mean when they use the term "sovereignty"? That is the question.'

I write notes as he speaks and at the bottom of the page I scrawl: Asking the wrong question. I underline it.

I still feel unintelligent and inarticulate – awkward – when I talk through my ideas with Professor Young. Nothing he says or does causes this; he constantly encourages me with attentiveness and reflection. The self-doubts grow from deep within me, sparked by my own insecurities. My father had been at the original Tent Embassy in Canberra and a well-known voice in the Aboriginal rights movement ever since. A lot was expected of Tony Harlowe's daughter.

Professor Young breaks the lull in our conversation. 'And what are you reading for fun, Simone?'

He asks me this question each time we meet so I've prepared my answer. '*Lolita.*'

'Ah, Nabokov. And how should we deal with his arch-villain, the urbane Humbert Humbert?'

'Well, Nabokov doesn't make it easy for us. He tells the whole story from Humbert Humbert's point of view so we are fed all his lies and excuses.'

Professor Young nods. 'That's Nabokov's genius. He makes us feel sympathy for a man whom we objectively would never like, someone whom we should find repugnant.'

'I know,' I agree enthusiastically. 'Throughout the novel, up until the point where he has intercourse with Lolita, Humbert has committed no crime. Lust is not a crime. It's not a crime to love someone we can't have. His lechery is *morally* repugnant but it's not illegal. The law won't interfere until a crime has been committed.'

These thoughts tumble from me as I speak even though they had not been clearly formed until now. Every time Professor Young asks a question it somehow prompts me to think about things in a way that I hadn't before.

'Nabokov shows that law and morality are a bad fit,' he observes.

We talk about the difference between legal wrongs and moral wrongs. 'The message in *Lolita*,' I say, 'is that it is immoral if we do not understand how our actions affect others. Failing to understand the effects of our actions on the people around us is not against the law but in the moral sense, it's a crime.' I notice I have started twirling my hair with my fingers as I have answered. I do this sometimes when I think. Suddenly conscious of it, I place my hand back on the closed notebook that rests in my lap.

Professor Young gives me a contemplative smile. I might have bombed on my thesis topic but I'm acing Nabokov.

'I think you're absolutely right.' He swivels his chair so that he is at right angles to me. His gaze drifts out the window. 'The only redemption we have is when we understand the way we have affected other people's lives.'

Despite his slight smile, I sense a sadness, a private sorrow that I do not understand. I love watching the expressiveness of Professor Young's face as he speaks but I can always tell when our conversation is at an end. He turns back to me, looks at the clock on his desk then nods at me. He stands and walks me to the door, ushering me out. 'Good luck, Simone. Just drop in if there is anything further you wish to raise with me.' I no longer feel like the favoured child; I feel like he will not think of me again until my next briefing note arrives in his in-tray in a month's time.

As I walk home I think of how much I loved *Lolita*. It's a story of seduction. Not just the seduction of Lolita, but of the reader, of me. Humbert Humbert tries to persuade us with his tale and the minute we see it as a love story, we have succumbed to his charm, have fallen into his trap.

My meetings with Professor Young give me not just clarity about my thesis but a new way to look at the world.

When I was younger, as we sat in the kitchen my father would tell me how he saw the world. He would talk to me as he peeled vegetables, turned sausages, or stirred soup. He would stop and wave his cooking utensils to emphasise his points. 'There was no treaty with Aboriginal people, the first people,' he would say. 'You show me where we ever handed over our land.'

Dad would give moral arguments. But Professor Young can give the legal arguments as well. He's the one who brings out the best in me now. There's a sadness in outgrowing your parents but I guess it happens to everyone.

2

As Professor John Young sat back behind his desk, he whispered the words again. 'The only redemption we have is when we understand the way we have affected other people's lives.' His nerves pulled within him.

When his daughter Lucy had died seven long years ago, John had felt as though everything was swimming in a different direction to him. His grief had spun around him and against this swirling tide he had failed to be an anchoring strength for either his wife, Louise, or his elder daughter, Jessica. Lucy had been eleven. The senselessness of her death swallowed him; his grief was an abyss.

After Lucy's death he had, by chance, met Charmaine and left Louise to be with her. Since then he'd been estranged from his only other child. Jessica was stubborn and unyielding. She never forgave his abandonment of her after Lucy's death and she nurtured a bitter resentment that he was now too frightened to face. He never blamed Jessica for taking her mother's side. And now, in dark moments, he admitted to himself that her unrelenting hatred of him was justified.

He recalled Simone's comment: *'Failing to understand the effects of our actions on the people around us is not against the law but in the moral sense, it is a crime.'* And Jessica kept coming to mind.

When he met Charmaine she'd seemed the only way he could save himself. He was selfish, possessed with such consuming grief, but Charmaine had been renewing, bringing freshness and hope back into his life. They planned a future together, a new beginning. He'd wanted more children desperately – another Lucy – and had thought when he married Charmaine that she did too. That's what she had said to him and he had believed her. She would lie curled up in his arms and he would tell her how beautiful she'd look when she became pregnant. She would tell him the names she liked – Jasmine, Tara and Chanel if it was a girl; James, Jackson or Jason if it was a boy. She would look at the Barbie dolls and children's clothes when they went shopping. 'So adorable,' she would squeal.

But so many things turned out to be illusions that, once exposed, left only the dust of disappointment. Her promises of giving him a child now seemed like a hollow lure. The sanctuary he'd felt in his marriage throughout its first four years had vanished in the last two. She seemed as disinterested in him as he was with her and, with no children, their large creaky house felt cold and empty.

The spark of rescue that Charmaine brought to his life was now gone. He could no longer bring to the surface the inspiration to write poetry, his once beloved release. The words that slipped onto the pages from his hand now were merely the groans of an older, bitter man. He would crumple the thick white paper, feeling vacant, as though icy hands had dipped inside him to crush everything warm and breathing.

Shafts of late afternoon sunlight were coming through the window of John's office, the warmth momentarily comforting him. If he closed his eyes he was back under the clear Italian summer sun, having just turned eighteen, falling in love. In those summer months he had felt immortal, fearlessly jumping from tall blonde cliffs into an endless turquoise sea. But as he reopened his eyes he felt as though he had always been acidly cynical, older than he really was in years, and the sun, no matter how hot it might get, did not seem enough to properly warm him.

In Simone he'd seen that enthusiasm so lost in himself, especially in the way she glowed when they talked about literature. He'd loved *Lolita* too, the lyrical way that Nabokov used language: *Lolita, light of my life, fire of my loins. My sin, my soul. Lo-lee-ta: the tip of the tongue*

*taking a trip of three steps down the palate to tap, at three, on
the teeth. Lo. Lee. Ta.*

He had forgotten until Simone had reminded him.
She was animated, her face alive. Seeing that light in
Simone made him want to reach out to her. 'Don't
lose this,' he wanted to say to her. 'It's far too precious.
Once it's gone, you might as well be dead.'

He had first glimpsed that shimmer when he read
a paper Simone had submitted for his class. Her writing had been optimistic, original. When she made an
appointment to see him, he matched the name on the
paper to the face of the young woman who wore so
many bangles to class that she jingled when she walked.
She had stood out, with her long dark hair and dark
features. He had assumed she was Spanish or Italian
and was surprised to find that she was an Australian
Aboriginal – the first he had ever met. He had felt flattered when she had sought him out, had wanted him
to work with her. He felt paternal pleasure as he saw
her develop her strong, sharp mind. He smiled as he
thought of the way she would twirl strands of her hair
around her finger when she was deep in thought.

John looked at the photograph of his wife framed in
embossed silver. Her long dark hair and exquisite tulip-
petal lips. Even though his love for her felt crushed,
he could not deny her beauty was breathtaking. He
turned the frame over, placing it face down on the desk.
Exhaustion seeped into his muscles. He had not been

sleeping well, lucky to catch more than a few hours a night, which left his days stained with fatigue. Once he had been frantic, untamed ideas spurting into his head. He scrambled to capture each shard of thought, prolifically writing his observations and opinions about law, power imbalance, injustice. He had been heralded as a genius by the age of twenty-five with the publication of two critiques of the legal system that had secured for him a meteoric rise within the elitist realms of his chosen profession. At the same time he had found a space – a creativity – away from the law in which he could compose his poetry. Now that man seemed forever lost. A ghost.

John looked through the papers in his in-tray – an invitation to a round-table discussion on Fellini and fascism, requests for talks, comments, references, advice. 'Please read this', 'please give your comments on that' – he left them all. Collecting his coat and scarf, he started the half-hour walk home.

It was getting dark earlier and the air had a suspended bite to it. He felt the light wind sweep across his face as he walked through the university yard, past the large brick chapel that was crowned with white columns and arches. For so many years it had seemed unchanged, he thought. John had gone through the ornate doors into the otherwise austere building on his first day as a student almost thirty years ago and it was as strong and solid now as then. He was the one who had aged from the athletic, understatedly handsome man he once was. His face still retained its boyishness but it was now carved with lines around his mouth, forehead and eyes; and the grey was seeping through his hair.

'Thirty seasons have come and gone since I first came here,' he whispered to himself. 'Almost thirty times I have seen these trees watch their leaves burn and fall to the ground, stand naked in the snow, scratching the sky, until budding with life again in the spring. A pity we don't spring to life again, renewed. A shame we only get one cycle and that we decay in the process.'

When John finally stepped through his front door, the large house was still. He took off his coat and scarf, hung them by the door and trudged to the kitchen. He opened the fridge and looked at the wrapped scraps of food. He did not know where his wife was but, if he was honest, he didn't care if she never came home. He grimly closed the refrigerator door, no longer hungry.

3

When I arrive back to my small apartment, I pour a glass of wine – Australian sauvignon blanc, a little piece of home. Instead of writing up the notes from my meeting with Professor Young, I check my email. There is a message from Tanya Randall, my best friend. Her picture sits above my computer. She has her arms around me, her dark eyes are dancing and her curly long hair is flicked over onto one side. The photograph was taken at a community awards night that had honoured both our fathers. We are in evening dresses, laughing.

Hi Sim,
Can't sleep. Terry didn't come home last night. I am sure I'll get another lame excuse. What has happened to me that I put up with this crap?
Tan x

I never liked Terry. I'm not just saying that because Tanya is my best friend and I think no one is good enough for her. First of all, 'Terry' sounds like someone who would wear knitted vests. It reminds me of 'Terry towelling' and gold chains and comb-over hair, the sort of man who would use his dead wife's frequent flyer points to take his new wife on a holiday. Terry. Terence. Terrible.

I was with Tanya the night she met Terry and I didn't like him from the start. We were at a fundraising event and he spent the whole time chatting to Tanya. At about two in the morning, when she went to the jillawa, I heard Terry tell his friend that he was going to call his wife. It was a good lesson in why women should never go to the toilet in pairs. You would think that would have been the end of that but a year later he was moving in to Tanya's flat. To my mind it's bad karma to steal a person from someone else. If a man will leave his wife for you, it won't be hard for him to move on to someone else.

But there was no telling Tanya. She was smitten. And she looked so happy. None of us had the heart to burst her bubble with our doubts. Now that his behaviour had become suspicious, none of us was feeling smug about being right. In fact, it only made me dislike him more.

Dear Tan,
Just ask him. Then you will know. Even if he doesn't tell you the truth, you will see it in his face.
Sim x

I've been friends with Tanya my whole life. Her father, Arthur, and my dad had both grown up in the same country town. They'd gone to the Tent Embassy together and Arthur was even with Dad when he first met Mum. I don't have much family, or much that I see regularly. Mum has rare contact with her sisters; her parents passed away long ago. Dad's sister died before I was born and now it is just Nan who comes to visit from time to time. So Tanya, being the same age as me, is like a sister.

We'd both get sent away to Wallaga Lake mission for school holidays and we would have to make our own fun. Living for a time with other Aboriginal people who had so little made us appreciate what we did have. I felt the loss of our privileges more than Tanya over those summers but she could always make sure we were never bored. One time she had the idea that we take the inflatable dinghy out to the island in the middle of the lake. We exhausted ourselves blowing up the rubber boat then seriously miscalculated how much we would weigh and had tried to get on board too close to shore. It wasn't until we were halfway to the island that we realised that our manoeuvrings had caused the rubber bottom to graze across the oyster beds, causing a slow leak. We had to abandon ship and swim back to shore. I still smile when I think of it. And how I laughed when I told Jamie about it.

Jamie.

I jolt as soon as his name slips into my thoughts. Once again I have broken my promise to myself not to think about him. I break this promise too often. There are times when I walk across the neatly trimmed lawns of the university and feel the tradition and privilege that seem to emanate from the stone walls and know that I have made the right decision. But there are other times, in the half-light of a restless night, when I feel the dread of having made the wrong one. My whole body aches for the lightness of Jamie's touch but I whisper to myself, 'Enough. Enough. Enough.'

I read somewhere that it takes half the length of a relationship to get over it. It has now been fourteen months since Jamie and I broke up after two years of being together and I still haven't moved on. According to the formula, I should have stopped moping four months ago. I've been on several dates – nice meals, a drive to see the leaves changing – since moving to Boston but my indifference always showed. It's hard to pretend your heart is in something when you have lost it a long time ago.

Jamie and I broke up not because we were angry at each other or wanted to be with other people but because I decided to study overseas. There was no conclusion, no end, to how we felt about each other. And every time I feel the dam breaking inside me yet again, I admonish myself. 'Enough.'

The next morning I wake with a wave of homesickness

and there is only one cure. I call my mother. I know that it will be late in Sydney, after 10 pm, but like most children, even adult ones, I am sure that my parents will be glad to hear from me even though they are likely to have gone to bed.

'Hello, sweetheart,' my mother answers cheerfully. 'How's my girl?'

She tells me how the literacy program she runs in Silverwater prison is going and I tell her about my latest meeting with Professor Young.

We talk a while. And then I ask to speak to Dad.

'He's not home from work.'

There is silence. I can think of only one thing that keeps Dad out at strange hours and it is the same thing that kept Terry out as well.

All my life I have been asked, 'Aren't you Tony Harlowe's daughter?'

'Yes,' I'd say. Then an enthusiastic person would gush and I'd hear all about how my dad was an inspiration, had spoken at a rally or visited their school on a day that they were learning about Aboriginal history and culture. How they had read his political speeches and they changed their life. Once I'd be filled with pride. But as I grew older, there were times when I'd been tempted to answer 'no'. Just like I'd be tempted if someone asked me now.

*

I fell in love with Jamie because he was as unlike my father as I could imagine someone to be. Dad's a Scorpio. The Scorpio Man is magnetic, mysterious, shrewd, jealous, possessive, vindictive and self-destructive. Martin Luther King Jr, 'Lucky' Luciano and Charles Manson were all Scorpios. By contrast, Jamie is a Cancer. The Cancer Man is intuitive, sensitive, domestic, timid, insecure and needy. Harrison Ford, John Cusack, Giorgio Armani and the Dalai Lama were all born under the sign of Cancer. You can say what you like about astrology but it sure seems to have figured out my father and my Jamie. Jamie. You can tell by his name – the softness of the syllables – that he is special.

So, how was it that I came to be so far away from this man that I still love? Two words. Patricia. Tyndale.

Patricia Tyndale is a close family friend. She has known my parents since the Tent Embassy days and I have always looked up to her, even if she still scares me a little. She's a formidable woman. When I first told her I wanted to go back to university to do some post-graduate study, she pretty much commanded me to apply to study overseas in a way that could not be brushed off. 'You need to get that experience. See the world from a different place. Learn the things you can't learn here,' she had said firmly.

Jamie agreed and they both had encouraged me to apply to graduate programs in the United States. I wasn't as sure as they were that I would be accepted but before I knew it I was on my way to Boston with a scholarship in my pocket. But what I didn't have was Jamie.

'You have to do this,' he'd said. 'If I stop you from going, well, you wouldn't be the person I love. You may come to hate me for holding you back. I would hate myself if I did that.' While he encouraged me to go, he also pulled away from me. 'But, Simone, I can't feel like I am in the back seat of the car. I would resent you. I have to do my own thing.'

So despite my protests, despite my pleas that it would work (there's email, trips home, he could come and visit), despite my insistence that I only wanted him, and even in the face of my threats not to go to Boston at all if it meant we could not be together, Jamie stood firm. It was fate that I should go, he'd said. I had to do it because I was a role model. He wouldn't stop me but he didn't want to have a long-distance relationship. 'It wouldn't feel right, after we've been so close,' he would say. 'It would feel like it was a second-rate version of what we've had and I don't want that.'

Patricia Tyndale had, as always, the final word. 'You owe it to all of us to go. You have an opportunity that we dreamed of but never had. We didn't work hard to change things for your generation so you could throw those opportunities away. Especially to throw it away on some man.'

And in the face of that, what choice did I have but to get on that plane?

Later that day the phone rings. It's my father. I calculate that it is 7 am in Sydney. He can tell from as far away as Australia that I'm pissed off with him. He has this annoying habit of being super cheery when he knows I am angry with him. It works on Mum much better than it works on me. Always has.

'What do you want, Dad?' I ask sulkily.

'Do I need an excuse to call my first born?'

At this I am supposed to say, 'But I am your only born.'

Then Dad says, 'If I had a hundred born, you'd still be my favourite.'

This conversation is our little joke but I am in no mood to go through the usual charade. And at this moment, I'm not so sure that he doesn't have a hundred born.

Instead I say, 'I had time to talk last night but clearly you had more important things to do. I'm busy now.' I want him to know that his being unfaithful to Mum is the same as being unfaithful to me. 'And where were you, by the way?'

'I was working back late on a case that may interest you,' he replies, still so upbeat he might choke on it.

I can just imagine the case he was working on and I bet she has long blonde hair. I ignore the implicit invitation to ask him more. The silence and distance between us seem to echo down the phone line.

Eventually he continues, 'We're thinking of running a case to challenge an Aboriginal being on the $2 coin.'

'Is this a joke? Are you mad?' My anger with him rushes into my voice.

'There is a very clever argument about the fact that all the other coins have animals on them and then they put . . .'

'They have the Queen's head on them. And besides, that is not a legal argument. It's a political argument – and a pretty silly one at that. Not clever at all.'

I imagine that such a stupid argument came from the blonde who I've already pictured in my mind. I'm hoping my ridiculing of this argument will make clear my disapproval of her. That's my intention anyway. Besides, it *is* a stupid idea.

'Well, we will run it to make a political point.'

'What political point? That you are wasting Legal Service money on a case that will be thrown out on first instance? There is no action in tort or defamation. You haven't even got standing.'

'You think too much like a lawyer, Simone.'

I could tell he was getting defensive.

'I went to law school for five years precisely so I

could do that,' I say tartly. 'Anyway, I said I was busy, Dad. I have to go.'

I was already looking for an excuse to come home when the phone rings again. This time it is Tanya.

4

SYDNEY, AUSTRALIA

I have the window seat so I can see the southern suburbs of Sydney lit by the early morning sun as we land.
I grab a bottle of Mum's favourite perfume, some cigarettes (for Patricia Tyndale), and a bottle each of Vodka
and Cointreau (for cocktails with Tanya) at the duty
free before going through Immigration and Customs.

I direct the cab to Tanya's flat. It has a view of
Clovelly Beach. As I walk through her door, Tanya
eyes my duty free. 'We can put that to good use,' she
says.

I drop my bags in her hallway and notice that there is
mucky white stuff stuck to the back of the front door. I
look at Tanya for an explanation. 'I threw his dinner at
him. It's mashed potato,' she shrugs. 'The chicken and
bok choy didn't stick as well.'

We walk down the hill to the little cafés. It is almost
nine o'clock by the time our breakfast arrives.

'You look pale,' I tell Tanya as she stares at her food.

She looks up at me with a weak smile. 'That is a terrible thing to say to an Aborigine.'

We scan the beach from where we are sitting. There are plenty of people around, those who do not need or do not want to work.

'Are you going to tell me about it?' I understand Tanya so well and know now is the time to ask her about Terry.

'Well,' she starts, 'you told me that by asking him outright I would know if something was wrong. So I asked him what he was doing out so late, did he think I was stupid? And he said, "If you must know, I have been seeing someone else." Like I was asking for it, you know?' She bites her lip. She looks away for a moment, then turning her gaze back to me, she continues, 'And it turns out it is some barmaid from the Crown. That's when I threw the meal I had cooked for him the night before. He ducked and it sprayed all over the wall. "Well," he said very coolly, "if that's how you want it, I guess I'll leave." As though I was the one humping some young chicky after the pub closed!'

'Oh, Tanya. I'm so sorry.'

'And that was it. He left. He said he was in love with Tiffany – that's her name, can you believe it?'

'Coward,' I say. 'He's a coward.'

'He didn't have the guts to tell me himself that he was a two-timing rat bastard. I had to figure it out for myself. And then he uses my anger as the excuse to leave. I've just finished stuffing all his clothes into plastic garbage bags and I'm going to put them on the front porch.'

'Men,' I say. 'They're all the same.' Tanya and I continue to scan the beach watching a jogger run by, a couple walking their dog, mothers and their small armies of children. I think again of my father and our last conversation. 'You know, I think my dad is having an affair too. He's not home when I call late at night. From time to time I hear these whispers, snippets of rumours, innuendo. Enough to make me suspect but not enough evidence to say for sure.'

'There's something about your dad,' Tanya says with a teary, wry smile. 'You know what? I have to admit, I've always fancied him. Tall, dark, handsome, passionate . . .'

'Tanya!' I hit her arm playfully and give her a pretend-angry look.

'Don't worry. Your mother is the only person who could put up with him. She's a saint. I once saw a documentary about lions and how there is an alpha male in each of the prides who the female lions are all attracted to. There were also beta males, other males who were happy enough to just follow the alpha males. Your dad's an alpha male and you can't be near him without at least a fleeting sense of being secure and safe.'

'Well, that may be but if women throw themselves at him, he doesn't have to respond. Jamie wouldn't have.'

'Yes. Now Jamie is definitely a beta male.' I wonder if I've just detected a weary sigh in her voice. 'But I thought we weren't going to talk about him anymore,' she quickly adds.

It is one in the afternoon before I open the door to my parents' house. I quietly put my bags down and walk towards the back where I can hear the radio playing. Mum is seated at the kitchen table, working. She looks soft with her blonde hair looped in a loose bun. Gentle, innocent, like her name – Beth Ann. She peers at me through her glasses as I walk in as though she is waiting for her eyes to adjust.

'Darling,' she cries, shocked, when she finally believes that it is actually me standing before her. 'What are you doing here?'

'I thought I'd surprise you.'

She rises and rushes to embrace me. 'I can't believe it's you.' She pulls away and looks at me again. 'Why didn't you tell me you were coming home?'

'You completely stress out when I fly so I thought I'd save you the anxiety. I hoped it would be a nice surprise for you. And Dad.'

'Your father's at work but he'll be so thrilled to see you.'

'Yeah,' I say dismissively, but she plants the seed in my head that I should wander over to the Legal Service and surprise him in person.

But first I let Mum make me a sandwich. She also sets out two Tim Tams ('one for each hand') for me on a little matching saucer. Just like when I was a kid. It makes me realise how much I miss her fussing over me when I am so far away.

She fills me in on things that have happened since I've been away, tells me Mrs O'Conner over the road had been rushed to hospital, Annie Davies her colleague from the prison literacy program finally got engaged to 'that nice schoolteacher', Nan was promising to come for a visit soon, my cousin Erin is pregnant – again. These are the events that keep her world turning and, as I listen, I think how little everything has really changed since I was last sitting in Mum's kitchen listening to all her news. I want to interrupt her and tell her that I went to see Spike Lee and Oliver Stone talk about film-making, that I've done a creative writing class with Joyce Carol Oates and that since I read Mary Douglas's *How Institutions Think* I have not thought of law reform in the same way. But I am silent and smile at her while I sip my tea.

After our lunch, Mum resumes the preparation for her class, apologetic because she has to rush. 'If only you had given me some warning,' she chastises and kisses me on the forehead.

*

The Legal Service that Dad runs takes up two adjoining terrace houses that have been renovated to make a single labyrinth. As I walk into the reception area I see Carol Turner perched at her desk. She squeals when she sees me.

'Hey, Sistergirl.'

She rushes around the desk and gives me a bear hug. I am almost swallowed by her size. She smells of talcum powder.

'Did you bring me back anything from the States? Something dark chocolate and rich. Like Denzel Washington?'

'No. He said he was going to leave it to Valentine's Day to fly in and surprise you.' I clap my hand over my mouth as if I've let the cat out of the bag.

She laughs her deep throaty laugh. 'Speaking of surprises, your dad didn't tell me you were back.'

I wink at her. 'He doesn't know.'

I walk down the corridor towards his office at the back. The walls are covered with posters from various educational campaigns. Say no to drugs. Say no to violence. Get your child immunised. Say yes to education. Demand a treaty. Stand up for your rights. I like the poster that has Patricia Tyndale on it, her arms folded across her chest and her eyes resting accusingly on me. The poster tells me to enrol to vote. 'We fought hard for our rights,' it says. 'It's your responsibility to exercise them.'

When I walk into Dad's office, I see a young woman

perched on his desk. She's on the side where his chair is and he is sitting down, leaning back, looking up into her face. He is animated. I am almost through the doorway before he notices me. He stands too quickly and the look of immediate astonishment on his face, followed quickly by the slow comprehension that it is his daughter who's just walked in, causes the woman to turn her head towards me.

'Surprise,' I say flatly.

'Simone!' he exclaims, and pushes past the young woman to give me a hug. I stand in his embrace, unresponsive. 'What are you doing here?'

'I decided to come home and check up on things.'

I look at the young woman as I say this, recall the way her body had curved towards my father and I give her my best disapproving look. She looks at me expectantly and I turn to my father. I glance at the fly on his trousers to make my point.

'I want you to meet Rachel Miles. She is the new legal officer here.'

'Hi,' she says, holding out her hand. I take it limply.

'You came and spoke to our Indigenous People and the Law class about the Stolen Generations. I thought your talk was insightful. Inspiring.' She is not gushing when she says this, not patronising. She has long dark hair and, I grudgingly admit, is captivating to look at. Her intelligence shows clearly on her face. In other circumstances, I might have really liked her.

'Well, what are you up to, Dad?' I say, hoping that he will understand the accusation.

'I'll leave you two to catch up then,' Rachel says as she leaves, giving my father an extra moment to compose himself before he answers me.

I stare at her as she walks away, down the hall.

'I'm glad you're here, Princess,' Dad says. 'How's my first born?'

I ignore his attempt at playful banter and keep staring at Rachel's receding form. When she turns the corner at the end of the hall, I slowly turn towards him with my eyebrows raised.

'She's a good kid,' he says, as though I was cranky with her, not him. 'And you of all people should be happy that we can finally recruit Aboriginal people into the legal officer positions.'

5

'The problem with children,' Tony Harlowe said to Carol Turner, 'is that they grow up and learn how to talk. And then learn how to answer back.'

'Well, children are just a reflection on their parents,' she replied, one hand resting on her desk, the other on her hip. 'I always say, you breed 'em, you feed 'em. And you reap what you sow.'

'You seem to have no shortage of clichés up your sleeve and you don't have any children.'

'Well, I just haven't found the right genetic material to breed with yet. Not through want of trying, mind you, but it seems as though a girl has to kiss a lot of frogs before she finds a handsome prince these days. And I mean a lot. Anyway, you are proud of that daughter of yours. You must have done something right.'

Tony looked at her and smiled. 'To tell you the truth, I was just glad she didn't get herself knocked up before she finished high school like all her cousins did. Everything after that has been a bonus.'

'Yeah. Right.' Carol smiled back. 'That's why you are so good at weaving the "H" word into a conversation.'

'What do you mean?'

'Well, like you say, "My daughter – who is studying at Harvard – bought me this for my birthday." Or, "Carol, what is my next appointment, because my daughter is studying at Harvard and I need to be free before she calls." ' Carol gave Tony a smug look.

'Carol, what is my next appointment, because my daughter – who is studying at Harvard – has turned into a right pain in my ass and I need to be free as soon as I can so I can return home so she can continue to patronise me.' He looked smugly back.

Carol laughed and checked her computer screen. 'You have an appointment at four o'clock with a Darren Brown. Wants to talk to you about the Tent Embassy.'

Tony walked back to his office. How rapidly time had passed since Simone was just a little girl, playing under the tables when he was chairing a meeting or delivering a speech. She would sit in the kitchen while he cooked and he'd talk to her about invasion, dispossession, stolen children, stolen wages, Aboriginal sovereignty, all kinds of things. She would hang onto his every word, adoringly.

The next thing she was starting law school, then she was graduating. He thought sometimes he would explode with the pride of seeing her, at how he had made something so beautiful. But clever. So very clever. And that was even before she got accepted to Harvard University.

Carol was right. Since then, every second word from his mouth was 'Harvard'. But what he couldn't say – not to anyone, especially not to someone like Carol who seemed so quick to see his imperfections – was that since Simone had been there, since she had achieved this success, she had seemed to have grown disdainful of him, to see him as flawed. She constantly implied that she was disappointed in him.

She had always been a strange creature to him – sophisticated and, he had to admit, spoilt. If he had met a girl like Simone when he was young, he would not have known what to say around her. She spoke French and Spanish, talked on and on about designer this and designer that, attended fancy exhibition openings. She would scoff at the way he ate his scrambled eggs with tomato sauce or roll her eyes at him when he suggested they go fishing. 'They have these things called shops, Dad, so you can just buy the fish,' she would say, her hands on her hips. And at those moments he would be struck by how she had her mother's nose and chin, but unmistakably, undeniably, his eyes, his full mouth and his defiance.

He had protected her from the harshest aspects of life, the things he had seen, had endured, growing up in a small country town full of hate. He thought he had saved her from the bitterness that racism could give you. He had not intended to spoil her, had sent her to spend time with people who didn't have the advantages she had, so she would have some perspective. So she would know something of life, not be ignorant of the hardship, of the existence he had left behind, of what he had saved her from.

When he gave her lessons in history and politics, this creature he loved more than any other, he felt as though he was trying to impress her. When she looked up at him in those days he felt a pride that made him feel flushed. But she had not looked at him that way for a very long time.

Darren Brown was a handsome young man, with eager eyes, a strong chin and his dark hair pulled back into a thick ponytail. Tony thought he looked like a candidate for Carol's quest for 'good genetic material' and made a note to tease her about it later.

'It's such an honour to meet you, sir,' Darren gushed. 'My family are Gamillaroi people from Brewarrina.'

'Please, call me Tony and take a seat,' he replied with a magnanimous sweep of his hand. Tony felt comfortable in the position of mentor and benefactor.

'I believe you have come up from the Embassy in Canberra.'

'Yes, I've been there for a few months. I have to say, you are one of the reasons I went there in the first place. I heard you speak at the Invasion Day rally. I had been studying law – well, I'm still enrolled but I have taken leave this year – and what you said just made so much sense. More sense than anything that I was reading at uni, you know?'

'Well,' Tony said, using another of his standard lines. 'The white man's law is all about power relations and built on the lies of colonisation.'

Tony had always known how to read an audience. It was a gift, one that had served him well most of his days, especially after the Tent Embassy when he became a vocal advocate for the rights of his people. He could sense the audience getting caught up in what he was saying, seemed to know intuitively just what they wanted to hear.

Darren Brown, the young Aboriginal law school drop-out was his target demographic. Tony felt rejuvenated just seeing the look of reverence and animation that Simone had once worn on another young face. He settled back comfortably into his chair.

'So, what did you want to talk to me about then?'

'We are trying to get heritage listing for the Tent Embassy. I need to pull together as much information as I can so I can prepare the proposal. So I guess I thought I could interview you now, ask a few questions and, if that's okay, come back again for some follow-ups.'

'Sure,' replied Tony. 'Whatever you need.'

'Great,' Darren smiled. And then, looking serious, 'It's such an honour to get this chance to talk to you.'

'Well, I'm not sure about that,' responded Tony, attempting modesty. 'But before you ask away, let me tell you something.'

Aware that Darren was hanging onto his every word, pen poised and writing pad ready, Tony paused for effect. 'The first thing you need to appreciate,' he continued, 'is that the Tent Embassy was the culmination of all the work that had gone on from the 1880s through to the 1930s and beyond to improve the lives of Aboriginal people. But, at the same time, it was the beginning of the modern land rights movement as well.'

Tony leaned a little further back in his chair. Darren, with brow furrowed, scribbled quickly.

'You see,' Tony continued, 'what we did at the Tent Embassy had its intellectual beginnings in the work of men like Fred Maynard, William Cooper and William Ferguson. They were men who worked on the land. They wanted to know why they were stopped from earning their own livelihood, from owning the land themselves when they worked as hard as any white person. They argued for citizenship rights – equal rights – because they had grown up unable to earn equal wages, unable to apply for the same level of financial support as white people when they were unable to find employment, even needing to apply for permission to move from the reserve and to marry.'

Tony watched as Darren tried to write down everything he was saying and paused to give the lad time to catch up.

'These men, the Maynards and Coopers and the like, they were self-educated men and their Australia was one that was riddled with the inability to enjoy the basic rights and freedoms that all other Australians enjoyed unquestioningly: the right to family, the right to livelihood, freedom of movement, freedom of speech, freedom from racial discrimination.'

Tony was working himself up speaking on one of his favourite themes. He spoke about the way leaders like Maynard and Cooper had believed that Aboriginal people, through their own hard work and initiative, could improve their own socio-economic circumstances and shake off their poverty.

'What do you think William Cooper would think if he saw the state of Aboriginal communities and families across Australia today?' Darren asked, looking up as he hunched over his notepad.

'Hmmm, good question. Well, I'd guess he'd probably be impressed by the way in which our people have gained access in the last three decades to many opportunities that were unthinkable previously. In Cooper's day, who'd have thought we would have the numbers of Aboriginal graduates from high schools and universities that we have now. We've seen more and more Aboriginal people become nurses, teachers, lawyers, doctors, accountants, engineers.'

Tony gave Darren time to catch up. He thought about Simone, how his throat was thick with satisfaction as she walked across the stage in her graduation gown, the hem swaying around her high heels.

Darren looked up from his notebook.

'How did you come to be at the Tent Embassy?' Darren asked.

'I remember hearing through the black grapevine that these blokes – Billy Craigie, Michael Anderson, Bertie Williams and Tony Coorie – had gone to Canberra and set up a protest right in front of Parliament House. I'd grown up on an old mission and me and my mate, Arthur Randall, had hitched rides, jumped a train and even walked part of the way until we got there. Heaps of people had arrived by then.' Tony could see the images, the crowded tents and tarpaulins as they clustered together on the lawn. He could remember the pungent, rank smells of communal living. 'We were drawn there by the frustration that nothing had changed since the '67 referendum.'

Tony explained how people had organised, protested and advocated for the two decades leading up to the vote to change the Constitution in 1967, in the expectation that it would provide new opportunities. 'But we woke up the morning after and nothing had changed. We came to realise that we needed something more. The time for this movement was ripe. The moment had come. And I just knew that I had to be a part of it.'

When Darren finally looked up at him Tony was reminded of how strong the young man's features were. Dark eyes and thick lashes. Clear skin. Sleek lines on his face. But he could see something else in Darren, something in the intensity with which he wrote Tony's answers, with which he had devoted himself to something he believed in. It reminded Tony of himself when he was younger.

'When I was your age, I didn't have the opportunities you have now. You should think of that before you throw them away. Why did you drop out of uni?'

'Family things, I guess. My mother got sick and then I got caught up with this.' Darren waved his notebook.

'Well, the Tent Embassy is important. No denying that. And I know how it is with blackfellas and their families. But you'll be more valuable to our community and better able to provide for them if you get the best education you can. There's something for you to think about before I see you next.'

*

How easy the telling of this version of history had become, as though it really had been the truth. A favourite theme of his speeches, Tony thought, still sitting at his desk an hour after Darren had left, was the way white history was a fabrication, a story woven with lies. And the irony was that his own history had become the same thing. And while he had told the story of how he had been drawn towards the swelling activity on the lawns of Parliament House, the truth was he had been running away. Running away from secrets, dark secrets.

Tony had invented his own rules for survival back then, a list of five principles he had created during the rough and tumble of that trip to Canberra. He had scribbled down what he referred to as 'Tony Harlowe's Five Survival Rules' on the inside cover of a copy of George Orwell's *Animal Farm*, one of his favourite books, one of the few things he had taken with him when he fled his old life.

One of the rules was to stay in the spotlight. After all, if people don't see you, how do they know you exist? Everything is judged by appearance; what is unseen counts for nothing. Tony's intention was – had been for a long time – to attract attention by being larger, more charismatic, more mysterious than his rivals. Cicero once said that even those who argue against fame still want the books they write against it to bear their name on the cover. We will let our friends share almost anything, but nobody wants to share their fame or reputation.

For years Tony Harlowe had wanted to make a name for himself, had wanted to be someone. The first rule for survival he had written down was 'Be someone else'. And the Tent Embassy had given him a stepping stone from which to do that.

6

SYDNEY, AUSTRALIA

My meeting with Professor Young is still scheduled for 4 pm on the third Thursday of the month even though I am in Sydney. The time difference means I have to dial his office at 6 am. I have risen early, barely sleeping last night for fear of not hearing the alarm. I cannot help but smile to myself that I will be having a conversation with Professor Young while I am in my pyjamas; I am usually so meticulous about what I wear and how I look when I get ready to see him. My notes lie scattered across my bed.

Professor Young had not been happy about my going home. I had told him that I had to attend to some family business but he had not seemed very sympathetic.

'It's a mistake,' he had said bluntly. 'Every student I have ever known who thought they could do the bulk of their research and writing around the distractions of their home town has always found out that they can't.'

And I have to admit that, as with most things, he has been right. The pages I had sent him earlier in the week were cobbled together a few days before they were due. I had lost the discipline of the routine I had fallen into in Boston. Here in Sydney there always seemed to be other things to do during the mornings when I would usually be working on my writing and in the evenings when I'd be doing my reading.

I've spent plenty of time consoling Tanya about her break-up with Terry and this has required long phone conversations, sleepovers, shopping trips and going to the movies. I've also been catching up with other friends and emailing Jamie, who is in Perth for a few months for work and not due back until December.

And I've also been distracted by not being able to shake my suspicions about my father's infidelity. For the last three weeks, I've been trying to find any evidence of it. But he has had no late nights and my several unannounced trips to his office have uncovered nothing.

He has not always been so careful. When I was a child, he would take me to a movie most weekends – just him and me, father and daughter. It was our ritual – looking through the movie guides, making a list of the films we wanted to see, writing down cinemas and times, making sure we arrived in time to catch the trailers in case there were movies about to be released that could be added to our 'must see' list.

One day, when I was about twelve, we had gone to the movies and, it seemed by chance, ran into one of my father's friends. Her name was Liz. On the way home, my father said, 'It might be best not to tell your mother about Liz. Let's make it our little secret.' In my innocence I enjoyed the conspiracy of silence, seeing it as no more than a secret I shared with my dad.

The next few times that we went to the movies, we always seemed to run into Liz. I thought it was simply the strangest coincidence. And although I was sometimes tempted to tell my mother about this funny circumstance, I felt bound by my loyalty to my father not to reveal anything of it. Then, after several months, we saw Liz no more.

In time I began to understand what the arrangement had actually meant and how I had been used to cover my father's infidelity. How he had used, even abused, our trips to the movies, our special time together. I said nothing to my mother. I knew she would be hurt.

When I was fourteen I stopped going to the movies with Dad. I began to resent him. At times I couldn't listen to his political rhetoric, his talk about principles and human rights, all delivered in his self-righteous manner without reflecting on what a hypocrite he was, a hypocrite with a lack of morals. Especially when I compared him to other men who did not seem so morally flawed. Men like Jamie, who never gave me a moment's doubt. Men, I think now, like Professor

Young, dignified and intelligent, an embodiment of what a perfect father should be.

'Well, Simone,' asks Professor Young, his voice echoing with the distance, 'I can see from your briefing note that you have shifted your focus since our last meeting in line with what we discussed. What is your central argument now?'

'I have been thinking about our discussion. So, I've been reading what people actually say about sovereignty when they talk about it. You know, thinking about how they would answer if they were asked, "When you talk about being sovereign, what do you mean?"'

I tell Professor Young that I know there isn't much written on the issue that begins from the Aboriginal perspective, at least in academic discussions and debates. And when that point of view is taken seriously, it is clear that people are not talking about 'sovereignty' as we would understand it under international law. 'Listen to this from Kevin Gilbert – he was an Aboriginal poet and an advocate for the recognition of Aboriginal sovereignty – in a draft treaty he wrote with the Aboriginal Members of the Sovereign Aboriginal Coalition in 1987:

We are free to manage our own affairs both internally and externally to the fullest possible extent, in the proper exercise of our Sovereign Right as a Nation . . . Our Sovereign Aboriginal Nation, fulfilling the criteria of Statehood, having Inherent Possessory Root Title to Lands, a permanent population and a representative governing body according to our Indigenous traditions, having the ability to enter relations with other States, possesses the right to autonomy in self-determination of our political status, to freely pursue our economic, social and cultural development and to retain our rights in religious matters, tradition and traditional practice.'

I explain that I think within this concept of 'sovereignty' and ideas about the legal implications of recognition there is no claim for separatism from Australia but instead there is a desire to negotiate a better position within the Australian state.

'What does this "position within the Australian state" look like?' he asks. I imagine Professor Young, his eyes slightly squinting from the low sunlight that would be streaming over him now.

'Well, there is a strong aspiration for a capacity for decision-making, for community governance but there are a vast range of other goals: the recognition of past injustices, the aspiration for land justice, the protection of culture, heritage and language, to be able to access the same services and have the same opportunities that other Australians have.' As I explain this idea, I recall my father talking about each of these things.

'That's the next stage of your project, Simone. You need to map out what this "Aboriginal sovereignty" means to Aboriginal people and then map the pathway between where your legal system is now and where it should be going.' I hear a note of caution come into his voice. 'It may need a political solution at the end of the day, but even so you need to think about the role the law can play in that pathway.'

I had been thinking too much like a lawyer, I realise, but I liked the message better when it came from my work with Professor Young than when my father said it.

'I know that you were skeptical about how much I would get done here,' I say to Professor Young, 'but I think with this as the new focus of my research, it may be fortuitous that I am back here in Australia.'

'Hmmmm. My warning about the dangers of attempting to do your project away from the school still stands. You have the opportunity to work at one of the world's greatest law schools without distraction. Have the family matters you wanted to attend to resolved themselves?'

'Yes. Yes they have. And I will be making plans to come back in the next week or so.' I wince a little, knowing that is not quite the truth.

There is silence, long enough to express disapproval. And then I hear Professor Young sigh.

'And what are you reading, Simone?'

I imagine his mannerisms, his facial expressions, the way he tilts his chair sideways so that he can look out the window that is usually behind him as he talks to me.

'I have just finished Kazuo Ishiguro's *The Remains of the Day*,' I tell him. I don't add that I only finished it last night, knowing Professor Young would ask me this question. He always does. Even if I'm tempted to just watch a movie and bluff, I always read a book. But I got caught up in this one and reading it had not been a chore.

The novel tells the story of an English butler, Stevens, who dedicates his life to the service of Lord Darlington. It had promised to be a love story and begins with Stevens receiving a letter from Miss Kenton, the former housekeeper at Darlington Hall, alluding to her unhappy marriage. Darlington Hall has just changed owners and Stevens has a new employer, the wealthy American Mr Farraday. Stevens, under the pretext of seeing if he can offer Miss Kenton – now Mrs Benn – her old position back, accepts Mr Farraday's offer of taking a 'motoring holiday'.

It emerges that Stevens and Miss Kenton, when working together during the years leading up to World War II, had an attachment that bordered on romantic – always implied but never declared – as they shared intimate moments such as taking tea and talks at the end of the day. Stevens's inability to express his feelings to the more passionate Miss Kenton eventually led her to accept a marriage proposal from Mr Benn.

Lord Darlington was a Nazi sympathiser. In the aftermath of the war he is disgraced for his naivety in dealing with the Nazis before hostilities broke out and for his hopes of brokering a deal between Hitler's Germany and Great Britain. Stevens had been totally loyal to Lord Darlington, as any good butler would have been but he seems incapable of believing his master could be wrong in his politics and actions.

Miss Kenton has now been married for over twenty years and while her relationship with her husband has not always been easy or happy, she has grown to love him in her own way. With the arrival of a grandchild she chooses to stay with her family rather than return to Darlington Hall and Stevens returns there alone.

'And what did you think?' Professor Young asks.

'At the end of the book Miss Kenton has a family, even though she is not always happy and her family life is not perfect. Her husband loves her even if he does let her down but, sadly, Stevens has none of that. Instead he sacrificed his life to the service of a man who was morally flawed and eventually disgraced. What did he have to show for all the hard work, the loyalty?'

We talk about the importance of work/life balance as I bundle up my notes from the meeting. I lie back on my bed, looking at the ceiling, and listen to Professor Young.

'People didn't have as much choice in those days though, did they? If you got married, you pretty much had to leave your employment. Domestic service in someone else's house certainly wasn't conducive to having a family of your own.'

'You certainly do get a sense of how much Stevens has sacrificed the night of the large banquet when his father is dying but he continues to attend to his duties as Lord Darlington attempts to play statesman,' I add.

When I finally put the phone down I have a renewed enthusiasm. Talking to Professor Young always inspires me. The fear I harbour in the lead-up to the meetings that he will be disappointed with me, that I will make a mistake, evaporates when I actually speak with him and leaves in its wake the adrenalin rush that comes from a challenging, fast-paced conversation in which I feel as though I am in the hot seat.

The next phase of my doctoral research is to start really drilling down into what it is that Aboriginal people mean when they speak about 'sovereignty'. And the best way to do that, I decide, is through a series of interviews. This would justify my staying here longer. Perhaps until December when Jamie comes back from Perth. Professor Young won't like it, not one bit, but I'll draw up an interview schedule – I might even be able to do a few in Perth – and then it will be easier to counter his inevitable protests.

There would be no better place to start than by talking to my father.

7

He scheduled his meetings with Simone so she could be the last appointment of his day. Today, he had missed looking at her as she spoke, seeing how expressive she was when she was confident about what she was saying, loosening the nervousness she seemed cloaked in at the beginning of every meeting. Even with just her voice to go by he could, through the nuances, imagine her face, how she looked upwards when she was thinking and frowned when she was listening.

His meetings with doctoral students had always been structured the same way. He would start by asking them about their project: 'What is your central argument?' This required them to think more deeply and assisted them in understanding their arguments more thoroughly than by just writing them down. But he also had the habit at the end of their meetings of asking his students about what they were reading, knowing the question forced them to read something other than the materials they needed for their research.

It gave him a chance to talk with these bright, young students about matters beyond their studies – about life, love, ethics, duty, values and politics. John had always been a prolific reader, an only child who wasn't naturally drawn to sport – more of a loner than a team player – and he prided himself that it was rare that his students would talk about a book that he had not read. He had even introduced a 'Law and Literature' course over the summer semester, much to the amusement of his colleagues but to the delight of the students. It always filled quickly with a long waiting list.

He liked his discussions about literature with Simone best of all. He understood her better by her reaction to what she had been reading. He could see her interest in recognising right from wrong, in social justice.

It was just like Simone to pick *Remains of the Day*, he smiled to himself, a book that raised questions of sacrifice for work, of exploitation of the lowest classes and too much deference to the upper ones. But at its heart it is a love story, albeit a doomed one. Not of a love unrequited but one which failed due to time, circumstance and emotional limitation. Stevens's role as butler, as a servant, made it impossible for him to have a fulfilling emotional life. Inevitably, he could not act upon how he felt about Miss Kenton.

But, John pondered, what if you do get the person you want? What if you do have love in your life and then you lose it? Had Stevens been able to woo Miss Kenton, it would have been no guarantee of happiness.

Charmaine had fascinated him when they met at a dinner for Noel Phillips, an old friend who had become a local political figure. Like most fateful meetings, it almost didn't take place. The tragedy of losing Lucy had left him wrecked. Louise was visiting her parents and had taken Jessica with her. He felt uneasy about his ability to function socially, had lost his confidence among people, but his loyalty to Noel and the kind intent of his friend's personal invitation made John feel obliged to attend. He had planned to go only to see Noel, eat something and leave as quickly and as quietly as he could.

John had been seated next to an empty chair and was calculating how long it would be before he could escape when Charmaine Edgeworth walked in and sat down beside him. It is the worst of clichés to say that his heart skipped a beat. It didn't really skip a beat, so much as beat harder, reminding him that he had one. Her face, the softness of her skin, her bright, bright smile, her sweet, chocolate dark eyes, the tantalising curves under her red dress, they all drew him in. She melted into his heart that first night.

But he realised now that he had seen what he had wanted to see. He had been so low, so paralysed with his grief, so engulfed with thoughts of falling asleep and never, never waking. No wonder he had created something to believe in, someone to save him. And why wouldn't he have hoped to find it in Charmaine? He could not have known then that beauty could mask such coldness. She was so much more sophisticated than Louise but Charmaine brought with her vanity, materialism and deceit.

When he had discovered the birth control tablets while he had been innocently searching her bedside drawer for pain killers he felt like a fool. Their conversations about her wish to give him a child, and the disappointment he felt with each failure over the previous years were a farce.

Charmaine, unaware of what he had discovered, continued for a while – 'We really should go to Aspen this winter. It might be the last that it is just the two of us', 'Let's look at baby clothes; they are so adorable', 'Madelaine, what a lovely name for a little girl' – and he could not say anything to her, did not accuse her but just looked at her, disgusted, as she continued the charade.

Eventually his stoniness seeped into her. She understood that he had unmasked her and they never mentioned children again. Without the promise of such a future, one of hope, and with what he knew of her deception, he began to fall out of love. Since then he had been falling back into the abyss that she had pulled him from.

John put on his coat and tied his scarf tightly around his neck. His in-tray was overflowing with letters, tasks, requests that he needed to attend to but it all seemed overwhelming.

8

The front desk is deserted. No Carol Turner. Pity. She's funny, larger than life, predisposed to wearing large, bright flowers on her black clothes, always has lots of gossip to share.

I realise it's about lunch time and I should have rung Dad to make sure he would be here. But since I have driven over I decide I should at least check if he's in his office before I head off. His car was in his parking space. No harm in trying.

I walk down the long corridor, again stopping quickly to look at the poster of Patricia Tyndale – 'We fought hard for our rights. It's your responsibility to exercise them.' Love it. She looks so defiant. So 'Don't mess with me.' And she's the only person other than Nan who stands up to Dad. I've seen it in meetings when Dad is in full swing, thundering, 'And we are not having these people come down here and tell us what to do.' Patricia will sit quietly and then, when he takes a breath of air, say, 'Have you finished, Tony? Yes? Good. You've had your say, now sit down and let the others have a go.'

Nan isn't aggressive like that but she is deaf and will get Dad on the phone and be raging at him about something and he can't get a word in edgeways because she can't hear him. Classic.

I get closer to Dad's office. The door is ajar and I can hear voices coming from within. I open the door slowly, too quietly for it to be heard. I see my father standing face to face with Rachel, the young Aboriginal lawyer, his hand up her shirt, resting on her breast. I can see where the fabric bulges from the shape of his fingers.

'Bastard,' I say and he turns to look at me. He is frozen with shock. He does not even move his hand.

'You are such a bastard.' And I give Rachel a withering glare for good measure.

I turn and march back down the hallway out into the fresh air.

9

I am so furious I'm shaking. I can't go home because Mum will know that something is up. I can't hide my moods from her and I certainly don't want to tell her what I saw.

I drive over to Tanya's. As she opens the door I brush past her. 'I knew it. I knew it. He's a fucking bastard.'

Tanya looks at me, puzzled, 'Who? Jamie?'

'No, not Jamie,' I stare at her, perplexed. And I see a fleeting look across her face but I am too determined to continue with my rage so I let it go. 'My fucking bastard father. He just can't keep it in his pants. I knew he was up to something. Though I guess that was a pretty safe bet.'

When I turn towards the kitchen I see that Tanya is not alone. Her father, Arthur, is there.

'Oh, Uncle Arthur! Hi! Sorry for the mouth.' I walk over and give him a hug.

He smiles at me, 'Oh, I've heard worse at Land Council meetings.'

I grin back.

I've heard the story many times, of how Dad and Uncle Arthur, who had known each other all their lives, had left the old mission together, hitchhiking, sleeping by the road, until they arrived in Canberra. Uncle Arthur was a man of few words but reliable, kind. His quiet decency seemed to have always been eclipsed by Dad's raucous charisma, his flashiness.

'Don't judge your dad too harsh,' is all he says and I put it down to his loyalty to Dad. 'Anyway,' he adds, 'I was just heading off.'

'Oh, don't go. I won't say anything more about Dad.'

'No. I was going anyway. And you two seem to have lots to talk about,' he says with a smile. He might not have Dad's charisma but I have always loved Uncle Arthur. Many times when Dad was pissing me off I would wonder what it would be like to have Uncle Arthur as my father instead.

He seems slightly frail when he stands and he walks slow. He sees me notice. 'Those old football injuries seem to be reminding me they are there now.' He stops a moment and then adds, 'Tell me, how's your mother?'

'She's good. She's started a new literacy program and she is really proud of it.'

'Your mother always had a good heart,' he says. And I am sure that I see a look sweep across his face, too quick for me to decipher it, and as I look more closely, it evaporates into the air between us. 'And don't be too hard on your father, my girl.'

I love how he calls me 'my girl'.

As Uncle Arthur closes the door behind him I turn to Tanya. 'I love your dad. I didn't mean to scare him off.'

'Well, you'd scare anyone when you are in this kind of mood. But he was leaving anyway.'

'I'm ready for a cocktail.'

'It's only two thirty,' Tanya replies.

'I've already had a four martini day. And besides, it's midnight in Boston so it's a very respectable time for my body clock to start ingesting alcohol.'

'Let's ring around the girls for a cocktail tonight but right now I'm going to make us some nice, non-alcoholic coffee with this espresso machine I don't really know how to work and we can have a chat.'

When she has managed to make the coffee I explain to Tanya what I have seen.

'Hmmm,' she concludes. 'It's pretty hard to figure out how that was innocent unless he was giving her a breast examination.'

'How can he do that to my mother?'

'He is who he is.'

'But that's just the thing. No one knows what he is like. All my life I have had to listen to what a hero he is. How he talks about the rights of the oppressed, gives them a voice. Do you know how sick I am of people telling me how wonderful he is?'

'Almost as sick as we are of hearing about Jamie?'

'What's that supposed to mean?' I am indignant, furious.

'Nothing, nothing. It was a joke. A not-very-funny one.'

I start getting agitated with Tanya but it turns out that I am the only one in the mood for a fight.

'I'll go get another coffee,' she says and our potential argument dissolves.

'What was the other woman like?' Tanya yells from the kitchen.

'About our age. Maybe a few years younger. But she looked smarter than to sleep with my father. It sort of seems like sleeping your way to the middle if you ask me.'

'Come on, I told you he was attractive to women.'

'Well, I don't want to be reminded of that. And seriously, he ought to know better. And he doesn't have to act on it.'

10

'I can't sleep,' Patricia said, when Arthur Randall answered the phone.

'How did you know I wasn't in bed?'

'I didn't think you'd mind me waking you up if you were.'

'That's very presumptuous of you,' he laughed.

'It's my way,' she replied wryly.

'That's the truth.' There was a pause before Arthur prompted, 'What's up?'

'You know, the usual. Too much on my mind. Were you in bed?'

'No. Was just about to head off though. Was thinking about my girls.'

'How are they?'

'Apart from being the lights of my life? Good. Teresa seems to be enjoying her new job. She's settled down. Tanya has me worried. She just broke up with that fellow she was living with.'

'I never liked him much.'

'I bet I liked him less than you did.'

Patricia laughed. 'You have me there. How's she coping?'

'She has her moments. I went to see her today. Tony's girl came in while I was there.'

'Simone?'

'Yes. She was in worse shape than Tanya,' Arthur said with a laugh. 'I suppose it's not funny but it sounded as though she caught her father in a compromising position.'

'What do you mean?'

'Well, I didn't stay for the details but she said something about her father not being able to keep it in his pants.'

Patricia laughed. 'So that's what the young people call it these days.'

'I guess so. Just what we called it in ours.'

'Actually,' Patricia said more seriously, 'it would be hard for a daughter to see her father in a "compromising position".'

'I know. I told you it's not funny.'

'It would be less funny if Beth Ann knew.'

Arthur was silent.

'Sorry,' Patricia said and quickly changed the subject. 'Hey. Thanks for being there.'

'Anything for you. And you were always there for me when Sarah died.'

'They were tough times.'

'I still sleep on my side of the bed. Even after all these years, it doesn't feel right to take up the whole bed.'

'You always were a softie. In a good way.'

'Well, maybe. But the good guys always finish last.'

'That's such a cliché,' Patricia scoffed dismissively.

'It's a cliché because it's true.'

'Well, I'm getting tired now. Think I might be able to get some sleep at last.'

11

Tony sat in the kitchen making small talk with Beth Ann as she cleared the breakfast dishes. She told him last night that Simone had called to say that she was staying at Tanya's. He'd been watching his wife closely, gauging her answers to see if she knew but he was certain now that Simone hadn't revealed anything to her mother about their encounter yesterday.

He'd been relieved. He needed time to concoct a story. He couldn't explain himself to Simone if she had confronted him straight away and he certainly couldn't say she was mistaken about what she had seen. Simone would be more aggressive if he told her she was wrong. When he added in Patricia Tyndale and Carole Turner, he had a lot of strong-willed, opinionated women in his life but he would rank Simone second only to his mother in levels of complexity.

He looked across the kitchen. Beth Ann's back was

to him as she washed the dishes. Her body was in better shape now than it had been when he married her. She'd been doing yoga three times a week and her body was muscled and toned. Even now, with slightly more weight, with wrinkles creeping on her forehead and around her eyes, streaks of grey through her blonde hair, she looked so much like the woman she had been when he had first met her in Canberra back in 1972.

There had been hundreds, and on the weekend, thousands, of people at the Tent Embassy but when he spotted Beth Ann among the throng he knew immediately she was the one for him. Her blonde hair, her soft face – like an angel's, he had thought – and her gentle, tender heart. He had felt then and there that if she would have him, if he could make her his, he would be able to become the man that he wanted to be – strong, looked up to, respected. Back then he had been desperate for her, had persisted.

As Beth Ann busied herself with the drying, he thought of Rachel. She had begun working as a lawyer at the Legal Service in July and he had started sleeping with her two months ago after a lunch – that had stretched from day to evening – at a harbourside restaurant to celebrate her first successful appeal. He had just given her a necklace to mark the anniversary when Simone had walked in on them.

Now, even after twenty-nine years of marriage to Beth Ann, he still could not keep his instincts for searching out other women in check. There was a time, when they were first married, when he could not have imagined wanting anyone else, or any other woman being able to match her. Yet, just after Simone was born, he found himself tempted and the first time he actually gave in was the hardest. Since then he justified his trysts with a 'what she doesn't know, won't hurt her' philosophy. He did feel guilty and each time swore – and genuinely believed – that it would never happen again. In these quiet moments of domesticity, when Beth Ann was engaged in those small tasks of looking after him, he felt the deep shame of his actions.

Beth Ann turned around to face him, as if she had sensed his thoughts.

'Are you home for dinner tonight?' she asked, looking at the tea towel she was folding in her hands.

Tony lowered his eyes, glanced at the now folded tea towel. 'I don't know yet, love. I told Geoff that I would drop around to the Land Council after work to go over a few things with him, sort some stuff out. I'll let you know.'

The lies slipped from him with the ease of practice.

'Okay. Well, do let me know.' Beth turned to hang the tea towel on the handle of the oven. The kitchen was spotless. 'You'd better get to work.'

*

Beth Ann waited until she heard the front door click and was sure that Tony was out of the house before she left her chores and sat down at the kitchen table. She could always tell. It was his attention to small detail, ensuring he had covered his tracks. His small displays of affection and attention could not mask his guilt and remorse. Yes. She could always tell.

Beth Ann knew she'd always been the kind of person that others overlooked or underestimated. Maybe it was her slight frame, her fair blonde looks, her 'niceness'. She looked more fragile than she really was. People tended to tiptoe around her if they noticed her at all whereas Tony had such a 'huge personality' he could capture the attention of the whole room. No wonder she had paled in comparison, been eclipsed by his light.

Being so often left alone Beth Ann had plenty of opportunity to observe other people – she noticed their body language, where their gaze travelled, the inflections or intonations of their voice. She looked for the nuanced glances and the underplayed exchanges that gave away so much more than they were supposed to.

She knew – from the way he couldn't look her in the eye when he was lying, his evasiveness yet over-attentiveness – that Tony had always kept secrets from her and she had always suspected what they were.

She'd seen the first proof of his infidelity a long time ago, about twenty years now. One morning, after sending Tony off to work, just as she was leaving for her day of volunteering at the prison, the school had rung to say that Simone had fallen from the swing in the playground and had been taken to hospital to check for a suspected broken wrist. In a panic she had rung Tony at work, blurting out, 'Tony Harlowe, please. It's an emergency.'

'I'm sorry. He's off on holidays for two days. I don't know how to get in touch with him but I can leave a message for when he gets back on Friday. Or can someone else help you?'

Beth Ann pictured Tony leaving that morning, his chatter about a busy day at the office, of the meetings that would fill his time. He'd told her he'd see her that night since she could never ring from the prison. She hung up without revealing who she was and, in a daze, made her way to the hospital to take care of Simone.

That evening, Tony came home as though he had just come from work.

'How was your day?' she'd asked as he walked into the kitchen, dropping his briefcase on a chair.

'Busy as usual. Having trouble with the housing office again and that new assistant I have is hopeless . . .' And he continued with the details of an imaginary day as Beth Ann marvelled at the ease of his lies. Finally he asked, 'Where's Simone?'

'In her room. She had a fall today at school.'

'Is she all right?' he asked, clearly panicked.

'It's nothing serious but I think she's enjoying all the attention,' Beth Ann answered, a slight chill in her voice, observing that he hadn't asked 'Why didn't you call me?' or 'Why didn't you let me know?'

The next day he prepared for work, put his lunch in his briefcase and said he was heading to the office. 'I'll be in meetings all day and too busy to catch. Best not to call but I'll see you at home tonight.'

He kissed her on the cheek, oblivious of how unresponsive she was.

She didn't confront him. As humiliated as she felt, Beth Ann kept silent. For many reasons. She knew how Tony would deny it, she knew how he would fight when he was trapped. He would get angry, indignant. And she didn't want to hear the layers of lies upon lies.

She'd never known how to argue with Tony and his denial would be a dismissal of everything she felt. He was so good with words, could dazzle people with his eloquence. She had no such skill. Tony advocated on behalf of his people; she couldn't even stand up for herself.

And, strangely, while it was left unsaid, unconfirmed, it somehow made her situation feel less real. She was deluding herself, she knew. So even though the hurt ate at her, she kept quiet. And she stayed – in the marriage, in their home. Even though her life felt less precious; even though she felt more worn, shabbier.

And on each occasion after that where she suspected, could smell, the infidelity – when there was elusiveness and secretiveness – she was crushed all over again, the wounds reopened. But still she chose to say nothing.

Over the years she had developed her own mechanisms for coping with Tony's unfaithfulness. She thought of Simone, what leaving the marriage, breaking up the family would do to her. Beth Ann would brutally evaluate her own behaviour. Had she been unattentive? Could she be more supportive? And through this self-reflection she would process her anger, suppress her grief, her shame and her distrust.

She wasn't the kind of person to go to a counsellor but she would do yoga or aerobics or pilates – some kind of activity that would give her time to reflect. She would think about all the good times she had with Tony. She would think about his good qualities – he was dependable, strong, made her laugh; he did love her. She would think about how much she had invested in him and their life together. She would think about what her life would be like without him, how difficult it might be with her lack of education and lack of skills to make a living to support Simone and herself. Tony would never be easy about a divorce that he didn't want. He could – and would – make life very difficult for her. And in the end, after weighing her desire to leave against the reasons to stay she would determine that her best option was to forgive Tony and persevere.

She did have moments when she raged. The anger would boil up inside her and she would let it go by throwing a cup or screaming out loud. She once even smashed her hand against the wall. Always when no one was watching. She was unanchored by the way her unyielding support, her unwavering belief in him, was still not enough to keep him faithful to her. But always closely tied up in her decision to stay was the admission to herself that somewhere underneath it all she still loved Tony. This was her life with him, for better or worse, and she had long ago resigned herself to it.

The one thing Beth Ann had always carefully done was to keep what she knew about her husband secret from her daughter. A part of her wanted to tell Simone, to let her see the man her father was but this was a fleeting, vengeful thought. She would never want to turn Simone against the father she loved so much. Whenever she spied them in the kitchen together, talking over politics and history, economics and law, she would feel deep affection for them both. Those moments when he was tender with Simone, she had loved Tony the most. Whatever his failings as a husband, he had few as a father.

Beth Ann made a cup of tea and opened the paper to the personal ads. Reading them had become part of her daily routine, not because she was interested in finding someone but because Tony would always take the front part of the paper and she would be left with little to read other than the sport, business section, crossword, comics and classifieds (which included the personals section). She got into the habit of reading the ads, a guilty pleasure, finding them pitiable in their desperation but strangely spirited in their optimism.

How brave some people are, she thought, to actually put themselves out in the public, to advertise themselves, like shampoo or luxury cars:

Woman professional, university educated. Bored by the earnest young men surrounding her. Back to square one in this Snakes and Ladders game of love. Bruised but still attractive.

Some she found funny, revealing the shortcomings that perhaps explained why the person placing the ad was so lonely.

Athletic male professional (doctor), not quite 30, seeks beautiful (preferably blonde) girlfriend. My luxury home, fast car and incredible personality await. Needs to have the qualities of a good wife and the proclivities of a whore. Women with flat chests and flat shoes needn't reply.

And often, Beth Ann reflected on how her own might read.

Woman worn dull with neglect seeks escape so she no longer feels insignificant.

It had been a long time since she had felt any optimism about love. To find the last time it had swept over her she would have to go back decades, back to the time when she had first met Tony.

How young she'd been then. So fresh, so heady with the freedom of having escaped an unhappy family life, of being caught up in the spirit of change, of being part of something that seemed to really make a difference, part of what felt like history.

She would tell the story of how Tony had courted her, had proposed. She had refused him once, and then refused him again. When he asked her a third time she relented. 'You won't be sorry,' he told her, holding her tight. 'I promise I will make you happy.'

But like most stories, there was much more to it than that.

Her father, Patrick Gibson, had married her mother, Virginia, in Stanwell Park on the coast just south of Sydney. He'd been a coal miner and she'd wanted a better life, one that didn't eventuate after she became pregnant with Beth Ann's oldest sister. Beth Ann was their third and youngest child – all girls. Her mother grew more resentful each time a new daughter arrived, as though each child sucked more life out of her. Her father had only wanted a son and pretty much as soon as they were born dismissed his girls as disappointments.

What Beth Ann's parents loved most was alcohol – her mother would become spiteful under its influence;

her father, more melancholy, enjoying his wife's unhappiness, finding her misery amusing. These domestic dynamics made for a house that was full of bitterness and emotional cruelty. It was perhaps not surprising that as her sisters became older they sought attention elsewhere. Both were pretty with their blonde hair, blue eyes, sprinkling of freckles and sun-kissed tanned skin. Quintessential golden girls in a beachside town, they were both popular and, with little supervision from their parents, wilful and wild. 'Those Gibson girls' her sisters were referred to in unflattering tones. Beth Ann was 'the nice one', 'the quiet one'.

Beth Ann had always felt uncomfortable with the stern glances from the older women in the town that her sisters would brush off with a flick of their hair. She was not as rebellious as them, was shyer with boys, avoided their company and attention. She would rather find a quiet place to read than sit on the beach and flirt. Over summer while her sisters painted their nails, went to parties and changed boyfriends, she would spend her time at the library and reading aloud to the elderly residents at the local nursing home. She became friends with some of them and her favourite was an old Aboriginal man named Murray Simms.

During her visits he would tell her about his time growing up, of going to find pippies with his father and steaming them in a big tin over a fire on the beach, his time working on the fishing boats up and down the south coast, about his wife from Cowra, and their search to find the family she had been taken from as a child, her too early death from cancer and, Beth Ann's favourite part, the stories his grandmother told him about the life before white people came, before the struggle over their land. He introduced her to the poems of Kath Walker and Jack Davis. Beth Ann read him the novels of Mark Twain and Ernest Hemingway.

While she read, Murray seemed to drift off and Beth Ann would wonder whether he was caught up in the story or back with his memories. She, in return, was given a new way of looking at the world around her, became aware of a history that she had not learned in school but that inhabited the same landscape she did.

Murray's stories also made her realise that there was something shameful about the way Aboriginal people had been treated, an injustice that had been swept under the carpet. He told her about the policy of removing Aboriginal children from their families, of forcibly being moved from their land, of going hungry, of mission managers, of kids not being able to finish school. He also taught her about dignity and patience, of spirited optimism not being crushed by bigotry and indifference. Murray passed away, dying peacefully in his sleep, the summer before Beth Ann's last year of high school but the memory of him and his stories, and the way he had opened her eyes about the silent history, stayed with her forever.

Her two older sisters had left home as soon as they could – Helen, the oldest, marrying her boyfriend the day she turned eighteen and Pamela, her other sister, moving to Wollongong and sharing a flat with her friends. Left alone, Beth Ann still felt she was in their shadow, especially with the leering from men who assumed she had the same morals as her sisters. And without her sisters' fussing and bickering, the lack of warmth in the house was even more apparent. And with Murray gone, there seemed nothing to hold her to Stanwell Park.

When she finished high school, she wanted to escape the house that was so empty of affection. She was accepted to go to veterinary school and intended to move to Sydney at the end of February when her course started. Just after Australia Day, she read in the newspapers about the Tent Embassy that had begun in Canberra, started by just a handful of Aboriginal people but whose numbers were rapidly swelling. She thought of Murray Simms and recalled how after hearing his stories she had felt something was profoundly wrong, unjust, but she did not know what to do to make a difference. This, she thought, might be one way to show that she cared.

So in the heat of a late January afternoon, while her parents were in the midst of a screaming match, Beth Ann had packed a bag and walked out the door, hitching a ride to Wollongong and then across the mountains and inland to Canberra. The sense of liberation, that thumping in her heart, the giddiness as she set out was a feeling she never forgot.

'Such a long time ago,' Beth Ann whispered to herself, 'but I guess it takes a long time to realise that belief and love have faded.'

12

'What have I got on today?' Tony asked.

'Something your wife didn't check before you left the house,' Carol smiled.

She checked the appointments calendar on her computer. 'There's that Darren Brown at nine thirty. He's a nice-looking kid. Seems smart. Don't know why he keeps wanting to see you.'

'Yeah, thought you'd like him. And he wants to keep seeing me because he is interested in my life, in my achievements.'

'If he was only interested in your achievements he should be finished with you by now,' Carol quipped, knowing full well she was walking a fine line when it came to Tony's healthy ego. She knew when to stop and softened. 'You have a busy day ahead of you, Champ. Back-to-back meetings until five so I'll just keep sending them down.'

'Okay. And Carol, make sure there are no unannounced visitors.'

Rachel had taken her suit jacket off and Tony could see the tattoo that ran all around her arm in an intricate band. He hated tattoos. They were bad enough on men, let alone women. He had always told Simone that if she ever got one he would disinherit her. But at this moment Rachel looked sexy, fresh, and the tattoo didn't matter. He leant with one arm on the architrave and sucked his stomach in.

'What's up, beautiful?' Tony asked, trying to sound casual.

Rachel looked up. 'Well, good morning,' she smiled, leaning back in her chair and placing her arms casually above her head.

'Did you miss me?' he asked.

'Nope. I'm getting sick of you already.'

She said this with a laugh but Tony could only muster up the weakest of smiles. Her teasing made his shoulders tighten.

'I thought we could get some DVDs and take-away tonight,' he said.

'Nice thought. But I've signed up to a lecture at the Law Society tonight.'

'Can't you cancel? We haven't spent an evening together for ages.'

'No,' she laughed again. 'We could meet later though.'

Tony began to feel the prickles of agitation. 'It will be too late.'

He walked down to his own office and closed the door.

It was not a rare thing that a beautiful woman would present herself as an opportunity. He had travelled a lot around New South Wales in his work as an activist and now in his role as Director of the Aboriginal Legal Service, giving talks and attending meetings. Women would often front up to him and tell him that they admired him or were moved by what he had said.

It was hard to be unaffected by admiration, especially when he was so far away from the comforts of home – from Beth Ann – and had only a chilly, nondescript hotel room awaiting him. It was too easy to give in to the temptation of sleeping against the skin of someone who adored him, someone who looked up to him.

His seductions would usually end in the faded florals of fibro motel rooms in sleepy country towns. Every so often a dalliance evolved into a romance that he would enjoy until the expectations upon him became too great. Then he would say: 'There is no future for us. I told you that I would never leave my wife. You knew that from the start. You have to admit that I was honest with you from the beginning.'

This speech he knew well. He could say it with tenderness, without revealing the resentment he felt when the excitement and fun of a tryst had transformed into something tiresome and difficult, something he needed to escape.

Rachel was different. When she had started working at the Legal Service she had inevitably become the subject of much male banter ('hot body', 'great legs', 'love to do her' were the more polite jibes), especially at after-work drinking sessions. Instead of joining in, as he usually would have done, he found himself defending her, wanting to protect her. He would get angry at comments made about her that he would have found funny had they been made about anyone else. Once he even had to suppress the urge to thump John Franks and was now plotting to have him dismissed after he insinuated that he had known Rachel intimately.

Tony had conspired to create projects that he could work on with Rachel and would find meetings they both had to attend. The more time they spent together, the more intrigued he became with her. She was more than just darkly beautiful. She had a sharp wit, a clear mind, a good sense of humour. She made him laugh and didn't seem afraid of him or even in awe of him. It didn't matter how long he had spent with her, he couldn't wait to see her again. When they had become close, when she had first leaned into him and kissed him softly on the lips, drawing back slowly as she held his gaze, it had felt magical.

Now he was more than smitten with her. Everything about Rachel seemed new. She seemed to respond when he spoke seriously about cases or politics, was constantly interested in what he thought. She pushed him to think about things. He found himself wondering why, with all her sweetness and smarts, she would want him. For the first time he found himself fantasising about a domestic life with someone other than Beth Ann.

He entertained these daydreams but never shared them with Rachel. He'd told her from the start that he would never leave Beth Ann. Rachel had accepted his terms, had never sought to change them. While he was clear about the boundaries between Beth Ann and Rachel it was easy to navigate. But now that his attachment to Rachel had become so deep, so desperate, he was worried that the lines would start to blur. Three weeks ago he had told Rachel that he loved her. He'd surprised himself as the words slipped from him, falling towards her before he could pull them back. It was the first time he had said these words to anyone other than his wife and his daughter.

Tony's thoughts were interrupted when Carol rang to say that she was sending Darren Brown through.

*

'You can go through now, my brother. Oh, and do you mind dropping these off to the woman in the third office along the way? Her name is Rachel.' Carol handed over a pile of phone messages. 'You can't miss her. It's on your way to the boss's office. Would save me the walk,' she smiled with a wink.

Several minutes later, Darren knocked on Tony's door.

'Come in,' said Tony in his friendliest voice, gesturing at the chair opposite him. 'How have you been, son?'

'Good thanks, sir.'

'You're not going to start with that "sir" business again. It's Tony. Call me Tony.'

'Okay, si-er-Tony,' Darren stumbled over his words.

'Where did we get to last time?'

Darren flicked through his notebook to find his notes, 'Ummm . . .'

Tony smiled. He found the nervousness in younger people when they were with him endearing.

Darren looked at his notes. 'Oh, here we are. You had been talking about how you got to the Tent Embassy. And the impact of men like Maynard, Ferguson and Cooper the generation before. And about the 1967 referendum.'

'Yes, well, you need to understand what life was like for blackfellas back then. The Freedom Rides that Charlie Perkins had organised in 1965 had really highlighted to many people the way in which there were two Australias, that while there was an emerging middle class for most people, Aboriginal people were living in Third World conditions. And in many country towns there was blatant segregation, like apartheid.

'The white people in the town hated us and there was always some campaign to close the mission down, especially when others around the state were closed and people had to move over to the remaining missions that were already overcrowded.'

In the town he had grown up in, Tony recalled, there was a separate playground for black kids and no expectation that they would be schooled past the age of twelve, whatever their capability. Even going to the theatre meant sitting in a different section to the whites. The pubs would not allow Aboriginal people inside – although they would sell alcohol at inflated prices out the back door to them – and shop owners viewed Aboriginal people with suspicion, sometimes refusing to serve them. Tony found these indignities humiliating.

'And one of the worst things,' he continued, 'was the way we were targeted by the police. Where I came from, the police would come from the town to the mission whenever anything went missing. The first suspicion was that it was the black kids. I remember how the police came and took five youngsters away for stealing from the general store. They were sent to reformatory school, as it was called back then. And later they found out that one of the coppers had been taking the stuff.'

'Did the kids get to come back?' Darren asked, pausing from his note taking.

'What do you think? But if you are a young kid and you are taken from your family and put in the place where you are being punished, do you think you will ever be the same again? Especially if you were innocent all along but no one believed you because you were a black kid.'

'Did you ever get arrested?'

'All the time,' Tony laughed. 'If we were drinking, if we were hanging around . . . you name it and we would get into trouble for it. The coppers knew us all. It wasn't a big town. They took a dislike to some of us. I went around with a white girl from the town for a while when I was a young lad, maybe about fifteen or so, and they certainly gave me a hard time after that. A couple of times they took me down to the station and tried to get me to confess to something I didn't do.'

Darren was spellbound and had stopped taking notes. Tony continued. 'One time I got pinched they took me to the cells and handcuffed me to the door and every time this one copper came past he would punch me in the guts or slap me in the face and say, "Well, you black bastard, are you going to 'fess up to it now?" And you know, the more I stood my ground, the angrier he got. He was going to give me a flogging but I said I would confess and then, when he uncuffed me, I refused to sign the statement. Well, didn't he get mad.' Tony laughed at the memory.

'How did you get out of that?'

'Well, when he said, "Now sign this," and I said "No, I didn't do it," he jumped over the desk and started to throttle me. And you couldn't hit back or they'd get you for assault. I just had to take it. Sure took me a while to bounce back from that one. And it was only a few months later that I left the old mission for good.'

'Must have been pretty hard in those days.' Darren was looking up, his brow knitted with the same furrow as when he had been writing intently.

While there were hardships for Tony to face, it was hardest for the older people. They had grown up with the mission managers who controlled their lives – where they lived, if they could come and go. They had to do what they were told or they didn't get their rations; they lived in dirt poor conditions and were subject to inspections to make sure everything was clean. 'And, you know, over a long period of time when you are told how to do everything, you can lose the ability to do things for yourself.'

Darren nodded solemnly.

'You can see,' Tony continued, 'how we needed something to believe in. And those people who set up the Tent Embassy, they created that. The time had come to take control of our lives, to have some protections and guarantees.'

Tony talked about the political leadership of people like Uncle Chicka Dixon, men who had understood how important it was to give a political education to young Aboriginal people to guide them. 'These fellows had given up on conservative politics, you know, hoping that change would come slowly and knew that we needed to do something more radical, something more drastic, to really get justice. You need to talk to these blokes.'

Darren wrote carefully as Tony listed the names: Billy Craigie, Michael Anderson, Bertie Williams and Tony Coorie. Gary Foley, Paul Coe, John Newfong, Sol and Bob Bellear. Gordon Briscoe and Sam Watson.

'They were all involved and they'll all have a different version of events. I was new to it when I arrived at the Tent Embassy but those guys had been doing the hard yards – setting up the Aboriginal Legal Service, organising the boycott of the South Africans the year before to protest against apartheid. You should have seen them.' Tony laughed as he remembered. 'They were sharp dressers. Slick suits all in black, dark sunglasses. Me and my mate, Arthur, we were just country boys, boys off the mission. When I saw them, I thought, "I want to be like *those* blokes".'

Tony paused. He had reinvented himself after he'd fled the old mission with Arthur that night. The horror could still cause a wave of black dread to wash over him, the images would still haunt him even though there was all that time and distance between who he was now and the events of that terrible, terrible night.

Tony shuddered to dissolve the memory. He looked up. He'd forgotten all about Darren. 'Sorry, where were we?'

The phone rang. It was Carol announcing Tony's next appointment.

'Well, that's all we've got time for today,' Tony said with a sigh. 'How are we doing?'

'I really need to get more information about its impact, its legacy, of what came next.'

'Make an appointment with Carol at the front desk,' Tony said magnanimously.

Darren was glad when the session ended. Not that he didn't admire Tony or feel privileged to have an opportunity to talk at such length with the great man himself but because for the last forty-five minutes all he could think about was Rachel Miles.

13

Rachel still shuddered every time she remembered Tony's daughter discovering them in that playful embrace. She usually wouldn't have been so reckless but the rest of the staff were off at a training day and she had thought it was just the two of them in the office. Being discovered by Tony's daughter made everything so much worse, especially as she admired Simone.

She never thought she would find herself having a relationship with a married man and was surprised at how easy it was to block out the fact that Tony had a whole set of other commitments, a whole other life. She had known of Tony Harlowe since she was at school. She had read his writings and even gone to hear him speak when she was at university. He was dynamic, captivating, the type of person who brought people with him. She had applied to work at the Aboriginal Legal Service knowing that he was in charge and, quite frankly, she believed in him.

When Rachel had begun working with Tony, she enjoyed the tension, the electricity, between them. She was acutely aware of the competition between her male colleagues for her attention – the aggressive, unrelenting suggestions and invitations. Once John Franks pushed up against her in the photocopy room. She could feel his hardness as he muttered, 'How'd you like to get this into you?'

His rank smell of stale cigarettes was as repulsive to her as his unkempt hair and sleazy smirk. 'As if,' she had snapped sharply at him, shoving him back but she was still shaking as she walked back to her office.

From the moment something happened between her and Tony – that evening of their first kiss and the admission of deep attraction – the other men stopped bothering her. All except for John Franks who had slipped past her in the hallway and muttered, 'Should have known you would only put out for the boss.'

'What did you say?' Rachel challenged him, but he only responded with a sneer.

In their growing intimacy, Rachel saw Tony's vulnerabilities, his insecurities – a side of him that others didn't see – and she was beginning to love him more because of them. His prepared speech about how he couldn't leave his wife had clearly been delivered many, many times before and with such seriousness that she had to fight to suppress a giggle. She had not expected him to say that he loved her though. He had seemed too tough for that. When the words had slipped from his mouth she could tell they were not rehearsed, not one of his corny, over-used lines. In fact, he looked surprised that he had uttered them.

Rachel had always been interested in Aboriginal issues. Growing up, she came to suspect that she had Aboriginal heritage herself even though she could not confirm it until she was enrolled in the first year of her university studies.

Raised in the inner-west Sydney suburb of Strathfield, Rachel's father and mother were both English teachers and her mother heavily involved with the Teachers Federation. When she went to high school she was one of the few students in her class whose parents were still together. She would joke with her younger brother, James, that they should form a support group. 'The secret to a good marriage,' her mother would say, 'is never to go to bed angry.' 'The secret,' her father would quip, 'is to smile and nod and say "yes dear".'

It was always clear to Rachel how much her father adored her mother. He would beam when she addressed the union meetings and his gaze would follow her as she took charge and busied around. Her mother's energy was the efficient whirlwind around which everything revolved while her father was the family's quiet, contemplative centre. Her parents were focused on resourcefulness and thrift. Her mother made all their clothes when they were young and later would buy outfits for them at the markets, searching through bins and racks. They would purchase all their groceries in bulk and her mother always knew how to spot a bargain.

But amidst this prudent frugality, her parents were demonstrably affectionate to both Rachel and her brother. They were lavished with affection and encouraged to pursue whatever interested them – for Rachel it was ballet, the flute and later the debating team; for James it was soccer, then football and cricket. Even when she did something wrong – like the time she and her friend Janelle were caught smoking on the school excursion – her parents would say, 'We're not angry, just so very disappointed in you,' and that would make her more ashamed and sorry than any other punishment that they could have meted out.

Both her parents loved word games and puzzles. Instead of answering questions simply, even everyday queries like, 'How are you today, Dad?' would be answered cryptically. 'Feeling very happy like the mountaineer who climbed Mount Everest,' her father would grin. 'I see, you are "on top of the world", Daddy.'

When she was only fourteen, Rachel's father began to teach her how to do cryptic crosswords and solving them soon became a ritual they shared. They had a pattern. The paper would arrive in the morning and they'd make a head start. They would look at the cross-word, read all the clues and make a mark beside them if they had an idea of what the answer might be. If part of the clue was an anagram, it was underlined (*A Dior creation in most homes (5) – Radio)*. When sure of the answer, it was placed in the grid. After school Rachel would look at it again. Her father would have a go at it when he came home from work and then after dinner they would try to solve the hardest clues, the ones that still eluded them. If stuck, they would take a break and come back to it later. If they could not complete the puzzle, they would look up the clue the next morning and see where they had gone wrong.

From time to time her father would slip a folded piece of paper into her lunchbox, a riddle for her to solve during the day. The note might say *'Over it Wilts' by Cheer Sick Lands* and she would have to work it out (an anagram! *Oliver Twist* by Charles Dickens, which she had just started reading). Another day the note might read: *'Honest but careless, famous last words.'* They had seen *Gone with the Wind* on the weekend and she knew it was 'Frankly my dear, I don't give a damn.'

She didn't fight often with her brother but then he tended to keep to himself. James had no aptitude for words or numbers the way Rachel did and instead was preoccupied with sports; he was naturally good at them, while she had no talent and even less passion.

When he was a teenager, he became even more with-drawn, more reclusive, moodier. Her room was next to her parents' and she could sometimes, late at night, hear them through the walls. 'You don't know what he suffered before he came to us,' she once heard her mother say, and ever since suspected that James was adopted.

It explained why her brother had so much trouble fitting in while she enjoyed the same pursuits as her parents. Although she resented the way her mother's frugality meant her clothes were not as trendy as her friends, she shared her parents' values and their tastes. She felt she was the 'good girl' while James was the 'problem child'.

The suspicion that James had been adopted planted a nagging thought and before long she began to question her own heritage, wondering if she had been adopted too. She was darker in her features than her parents, didn't look like them at all, and she would get called 'wog' or 'Abo' at school.

She found herself drawn to Aboriginal issues, always felt a deep sympathy for the way they had been treated and for the conditions that they lived in now. She wanted to learn as much as she could about Aboriginal art, culture, politics and history, and she could not but take it personally when people around her – her friends, for example – were not interested, didn't seem to care or were even hostile towards and intolerant of

Aboriginal people. How could you hear all that happened to them, Rachel wondered, and not be moved to care?

Her parents confirmed her suspicions about her own adoption when she was eighteen. She knew the circumstances would most likely be hard to face, that perhaps should be left in the past, but she could not help but wonder.

At university she did her Honours thesis on the role of Aboriginal women in traditional society, countering the dominant stereotype that they were subordinate to Aboriginal men, treated like chattels. This was a particularly important myth to dispel in relation to criminal law where defence lawyers used it as an excuse to get more lenient sentences for their clients when the victim was Aboriginal. She had looked at the cases where judges had made pronouncements about how rape was not such a serious offence in the Aboriginal community and she knew this was something she wanted to change by showing that those stereotypes did not properly represent the role – and respect – given to Aboriginal women in traditional society.

But the yearning to find out who she might be – what was in her genes? what was in her blood? – eventually drove her to make some inquiries.

In the final year of her studies, Rachel made an appointment at a Link-Up office, an organisation that helped Aboriginal people reunite with their families.

She met a case-worker, Robynne, and told her, 'I don't have any proof that I am Aboriginal but I think I might be. I know that sounds kind of crazy but I don't know how to explain it.'

To Rachel's relief, Robynne smiled. 'Don't worry. Lots of people say that. It's a gut feeling. And we often find out that they are right.'

Robynne helped her obtain her adoption documents and traced her mother. She also broke the news to Rachel that her mother, a woman named Belinda Ryan, identified as Aboriginal on her death certificate, had died when Rachel would have been about eight years old. Rachel wondered if she shouldn't have felt something the moment her mother passed away and tried to remember if anything significant had happened at that time, a sign that her mother had passed from this world to the next. Her instinct that she was Aboriginal had proven to be correct and this gave her some comfort against the strange, complex grief of losing a mother she had never known.

Rachel determined to use her law degree to work on issues related to Aboriginal people, her people – and the job at the legal service, working with Tony Harlowe, seemed just what she had been looking for.

Out of home now, she had a different routine and she liked the independence. She would get to work at 6.30 am and have her first go at the cryptic crossword, look at it again at the end of her lunch break and if there was anything left unsolved, take it home to ponder, even call her father if there was a really tricky one. He would do the crossword too and they'd exchange notes. She could tell by his voice how pleased he was when she got an answer that he couldn't figure out and the smugness he felt when he got one that she had missed.

Rachel used the crossword as a bit of a talisman as well, a touch of superstition in what was otherwise a very practical attitude to life. She would look for hidden clues in the crossword to guide her own decisions. On the first day she began working at the legal service there had been a clue: *Destined to capitalise for all the eternities* (4). The answer was *fate*. And on the night she decided to lean in and kiss Tony there had been a clue: *Admirer for millennium's six balls* (6). The answer, of course, was *lover*.

14

The red figures 3.17 beamed from the electronic alarm clock. John's sleep was sporadic, restless. His tired limbs were a tense knot against the mattress. He looked at Charmaine, lying with her back to him, the slender smooth crest of her body wrapped under the blankets visible in the greyish blue dimness of the early hours.

John slipped noiselessly out of the bed, his bare feet treading on the wooden floorboards as he passed down the stairs to his study. He switched the light on and sat at his desk. He took a silver key from a small wooden box sitting on the polished desktop. He slipped the key into the lock of the top drawer of the desk and opened it. He pulled out a small photo album and opened to the first page. Two neatly groomed, golden-haired girls in matching white dresses, sitting on dark blue fabric with a cloudy background. Angels in the sky.

He placed his finger on Lucy's face. Her beautiful smile illuminated just as it had the last Christmas they were all together. She had unwrapped and hugged her new bicycle with all the energy an eleven-year-old could muster. That same bicycle would mangle her body when she carelessly turned a corner and rode into her death.

Jessica was practical and reserved like her mother, intellectual. But he could see himself clearly in Lucy. She had been inquisitive like him, her thirst for knowledge unquenchable, reaching out for everything she could grasp, asking endless questions, always with new ideas. She was like the person he had been at his best, before his sense of self had been poisoned by Charmaine.

His eyes then fell on to Jessica, Louise's child. He moved his finger to her image. 'I thought losing one child was the end of the world. Now, it seems, I have lost two. And it is too late to go back.'

John gently pulled a leather-bound book from the drawer. He flipped the pages over at random, his eyes resting on his own handwriting. His words. His poems.

Once these lines poured from him, swelling inside him until he freed them with a fluid hand. He had almost forgotten that sensation, the heat that came with deep feeling, the zeal in every living word. He flipped the pages again, running his fingers over the fading ink and so-familiar words.

John closed the book and held it between his two palms, wondering if the energy and emotion caught in the words on the pages could filter back into him. But he remained immune from that world. He finally, softly, placed the book on the desk.

His last two conversations with Simone still haunted him. After their discussion about Nabokov he had reflected on the idea of how immoral it is not to understand the impact of your own behaviour on somebody else. And inevitably he thought of Jessica – so lost to him now but only because of his own actions. He had sunk so deeply into his grief over Lucy's death that he had been unable to respond to anything and as he wallowed in his despair and anguish, he was blind to the pain of everyone else.

Now he could clearly see how this had affected his other daughter. She had been neglected by him when she was just as devastated and uncentred by the inexplicable tragedy of Lucy's accident as he was. Rejected when she needed him most, she learnt not to need him at all and turned hard against him. He had tried in these last years to win her back but she resented his efforts as being too little too late. She had been fifteen years old when he left Louise for Charmaine and now, able to make decisions about her own life, she chose not to be around him, made it clear that she didn't respect him.

And that's why his last conversation with Simone Harlowe also haunted him. In discussing *Remains of the Day* they spoke about the great tragedy in the way Stevens chose a life of duty over a life with a family. While he hadn't put his work first, what he had done, in his smothering depression and desperation, was reach for Charmaine to rescue him rather than reaching for his family. He chose her over them. Charmaine's deceit about wanting children meant he had lost the promise of a new family and he had turned his back on the one he already had. Little wonder that Jessica couldn't forgive him.

'Would you like to come over for your birthday?' he had rung to ask just three days ago.

'No. I'm busy.'

'You should make time to see your old dad.'

'Why? You never made time for me.'

'That's not true, Jess,' he sighed. 'I've always loved you.'

'Not as much as you loved your other daughter and not as much as you love yourself.'

This was typical of the way Jessica spoke to him. Her hostility towards him made him feel defeated and deflated. And in the end, because he knew he had made her feel that way, that it was a result of his own failings, it made him want to disappear, to have all the atoms that made him float apart until they melded into the thin air.

He opened the lowest desk drawer and pulled out a large envelope, then searched for his address book across the desktop, finally locating it under a stack of photo-copied articles that he had been meaning to read. He opened it and looked for a newer entry. He copied the address under the letters that formed Simone Harlowe's name. He slipped his treasured leather book of poetry inside, opened the wooden box that had housed the key and pulled out as many stamps as he could find.

On a piece of paper he wrote:

. . . a loveless world is a dead world, and always there comes an hour when one is weary of prisons, of one's work, and of devotion to duty, and all one craves for is a loved face, the warmth and wonder of a loving heart.

He slipped the paper into the envelope.

After sealing the package with tape, John walked to the hall. Still in his pyjamas, he huddled into his coat and wrapped a scarf around his neck without letting the book out of his grasp. Once he had checked his coat pocket for his keys, he quietly slipped out of the house and into the night.

The walk to the post box at the corner of his street was no more than a three-minute one but the cold seemed to lengthen the time to twice that. John's body tensed up from the cutting chill, his bare feet numbed. When he reached the mail box he looked at the name written forcefully across the package. He brought the parcel to his lips. 'Never lose that passion,' he whispered. He opened the flap of the post box and listened as the leather-bound emotions of his life dropped to the bottom.

Returning to his house, John pushed his hands deep into his coat pockets, heard the soft scrunching of snow underneath his feet. He could see his footsteps in the fresh snow as he returned to the house, the only one who had ventured out on this cold night. 'I never could get used to this damn New England weather. Always too cold for my liking,' he thought. 'But it's no colder than my wife. And no colder than my own heart.'

John entered his house as quietly as he left it. Still in his coat and scarf he returned to his study. He searched through the still-open top drawer until his fingers found the small gun. He held the barrel to his temple as his eyes fell to the smile on Lucy's face on the page in his photograph album. Her name floated on his last breath as he squeezed the trigger.

PART II

15

SYDNEY, AUSTRALIA

I am lying on my bed pondering how so much has gone wrong in such a short space of time. My bag's already packed even though my plane does not leave until late in the afternoon.

It all began three days ago when the phone rang at 6 am. I panicked and my first thought was that I had forgotten a call with Professor Young until I realised the next had been scheduled for just over two weeks away.

Mum had reached the phone before I even got out of bed. 'It's for you, sweetheart,' she said as she came to my bedroom door with the handset.

'Hello?'

'Hi, Simone. It's Glenda Barnes, Professor Young's secretary.'

'Hi. Do I have a meeting with the Professor?' I asked, confused.

'No. I have bad news. The worst, I'm afraid. I'm ringing to let you know that Professor Young passed away two nights ago.'

'Oh God.'

'Yes. It's awful. Just awful. And such chaos. I only just realised that you wouldn't have heard. It's been on the local news here. It was so unexpected and he was so well known. So popular.'

'I don't believe it.'

'I know. Such a shock. There's a family service on Friday but the faculty is having a memorial service in the church in the University Yard in two weeks. Thought you might like to be back for that.'

'Yes. Yes, I would. I was coming back soon anyway but I'll definitely be there.' And suddenly I realised that I would never see Professor Young again. 'I just can't believe it. Was it a car accident or a heart attack?'

The secretary hesitated, then she whispered, 'We're not supposed to tell but, well, if you can keep it quiet, he killed himself. Shot himself in the head. Can you believe it?'

'No. No, I can't.'

When I got off the phone Mum was waiting with a cup of tea. She could tell it was bad news. She has her own kind of telepathy.

'Oh Mum,' I stepped into the comfort of her arms. 'Professor Young is dead.'

She didn't speak or fuss too much, just waited patiently until I was ready to talk.

'I just feel numb. I guess it hasn't sunk in yet.'

'Grief is like that. You won't feel it deepest until you least expect it. And then something little will trigger everything locked up inside you.'

She comforted me until I stepped out of her embrace.

'What does this mean for your studies?' she asked.

'I'm not sure. I haven't thought about it. I'll need to find a new supervisor I guess,' I replied glumly.

Who could be to me all the things that Professor Young was? Who else would understand me and my work the way that he could? I put my head into my hands. My mother hugged me again. 'There, there.'

'What's going on?' my father asked, coming into the room, sensing the mood. He looked at me, then at my mother, then back at me. I could feel his rising fear about what we might be saying. I savoured his discomfort until my mother put him out of his misery.

'Simone's supervisor has passed away.'

'That's a tough break, Princess,' he said sincerely.

I nodded.

'What does it mean for your studies?'

'God, Dad. You are so fucking insensitive.'

He looked stunned as I stormed off to my bedroom. I slammed the door. I don't know why I reacted this way, why his asking the same question that Mum did elicited such a different reaction. I knew he had been genuine with his sympathy so why did it make me so angry?

I decided to ring Jamie. I really wanted to talk with him, to tell him the terrible news, but his phone was off. Not surprising. Sydney time is three hours ahead of Perth's. He would have been asleep.

While I was lying on my bed, thinking about Professor Young, my thoughts drifted back to my father. Despite my current grief, the resentment I was feeling towards him wouldn't soften. It was a frustration I couldn't articulate. It was more than his womanising that was making me instinctively push him away.

I tried Jamie again but there was no response. So I called Tanya. She was heading off to work but we agreed to meet at her place that evening.

'What a year we are both having,' Tanya sighed.

We were sitting on her balcony, watching the sun creep slowly behind the horizon.

'I know. But I think you win. I wasn't left for a barmaid who is barely the legal drinking age. Mind you, finding my father kissing someone would have to rate high on any list of "worsts".'

'He wasn't kissing her.'

'No. He was giving her a free breast examination.' I turned to look at her. 'Why do you always defend him?'

'Why do you always attack him?'

'Um . . . because he is the kind of person who feels up the young women who work for him?'

'But he's more than that.'

'Yeah. You're right. He is more than that. He's a man who betrays the wife who sits at home innocently supporting him so that everyone else foolishly thinks that he is some great man when, clearly, he isn't.'

'No one's perfect, Simone. Look at all he has achieved.'

'Other men achieve great things without such personal flaws. Take Professor Young. He never slept with his students or had affairs. He was a man with integrity and wrote some of the most influential books on the intersection between law and equality. At least he could be reflective about the world. About relationships. About how human beings treat other human beings.'

And in the lull of my heated conversation with Tanya my thoughts ran to my discussion with Professor Young about *Remains of the Day* and the tragedy of choosing a life of servitude over a life with family. I felt again that familiar deep stab when I realised he really was gone and began to comprehend what I had truly lost.

'You always do this. You idolise men. Put them on a pedestal.'

'I do not.' I'm taken aback.

'You do. Except for your father. And your feelings for Jamie are the worst. He leaves you rather than supports you to go overseas. He moves to the other side of the country. He tells you not to call because he says it's too hard when really he means he hasn't got the guts to tell you that it's actually over. And you not only hang on to him, you treat him as though he's a saint.'

'You don't know what you're talking about,' I snarled. 'You always see the worst in people. The way Terry treated you has made you bitter. Jamie and I are different to that and you know it. And you know why we couldn't stay together.'

'No. I know *he* told you why you couldn't stay together. But I also know that you loved him – you still love him – and you didn't want to break up. You going to study overseas should not be a deal breaker if he really cared for you. He used it as an excuse. You just can't face the fact that he doesn't love you anymore but didn't have the guts to tell you the flat-out truth. And because of that he has strung you along. You pine for him all the time. How convenient for him!'

The white heat of anger surged inside me. I was too furious to speak, too bewildered by all Tanya had said to answer her.

I snatched up my car keys and headed for the door.

16

My bags are packed – including a copy of *Billy Budd*, Professor Young's favourite book.

All morning I have been moping around, turning my fight with Tanya over and over in my mind. It's three days since our tiff, the longest we have gone with no contact when we are in the same city. It's true that I still love Jamie, that I idolise him. But I also believe his decision to end the relationship had been selfless. Tanya was right that it was not what I wanted but it wasn't true that he had used it as an excuse. Yes, he had told me not to call him because it would make it easier on both of us but I could see the sense of that, even if I didn't like it.

I want to tell him that I miss him. I want to say: 'I remember how soft your bottom lip is when I kiss you. I remember how smooth the skin on your spine is against the tip of my finger and I remember the smell of your neck, like heat and sawdust.'

I called him several times yesterday to tell him that I was going back to the States but he didn't pick up his phone and I didn't leave a message.

Mum yells out that the mail has arrived and that there is something for me. I shuffle out to the lounge room and look at the package she has left on the table. The first thing I recognise is Professor Young's distinctive, determined handwriting. I pick it up and look more closely at it. Pressed on top of all the stamps is a post-mark dated the day after he died. And the stamps show that the parcel was not sent from his office or it would have been franked.

'What is it, sweetheart?' my mother asks.

'I think it's from Professor Young . . .'

Mum and I stare at the package in my hands. Slowly I open it. It is a leather-bound book. As I pull it from its packaging a note falls to the floor. Mum picks it up and hands it to me. In Professor Young's hand it reads:

. . . a loveless world is a dead world, and always there comes an hour when one is weary of prisons, of one's work, and of devotion to duty, and all one craves for is a loved face, the warmth and wonder of a loving heart.

'That's beautiful. What do you think it means?' she asks.

'It's from Albert Camus's *The Plague*. It was the first book I discussed with him when I became his PhD student.'

The book is old and the pages are worn. The leather is soft with wear. The writing, in faded blue ink, is Professor Young's. I flick through the pages, all written by him.

'It's poetry,' I say.

'What an extraordinary thing.'

'Yes. Yes, it is. But why would he send it to me? And look at this. It is postmarked the day after he died. And it's addressed in his own hand so he must have sent it off himself.'

'If he wrote all of these poems himself, this really is a precious gift.'

'It's more than that, Mum. I didn't tell you before but, well, he killed himself.'

'Oh, my,' she gasps.

We both look again at the note.

Once I have read the book from cover to cover, I begin again. But this time I savour each poem, taking time to reflect on every one. Although each poem is a singular gem, together they tell a story of a smouldering, dark love and a crushing, cruel betrayal. I cannot help but weep at the deep, poignant emotion. This facet of Professor Young, the life he injected into each phrase, word, syllable, letter, is a revelation. I feel misery about losing this John Young that I never knew, just as I am grieving for the one I did.

Mum is in the kitchen at the table working on her teaching materials. I think of how often I have sat in this kitchen and talked to Dad, excluding Mum. Why had I so often sought his advice and so rarely hers?

It is almost time to head to the airport but I feel the need to ask her advice now.

'I have a problem and I don't know what to do.'

She stops writing and looks up at me.

'It's this,' I say as I place the book on the table. 'I am flattered that Professor Young sent it to me and all but it's such a personal gift. There are some very . . . personal emotions in here. And it is quite old. He must have kept it for many years.'

'He must have wanted you to have it.'

'But so close to his . . . you know . . . he couldn't have been thinking clearly. And it seems like such an extravagant gift too. Surely his family would want it. There's something unsettling about having it.'

'Of course it feels strange, given the circumstances. Is there anyone in his family you could ask about it?'

'Not really. I've never met his wife or his daughter. And maybe they will be upset that something so precious was sent to me instead of given to them.'

'Well, if you feel that strongly about it you can only ask. If they are upset, just remember that they are angry about *his* decision not *at* you.'

'You know, his ex-wife is on the faculty. Maybe I could go and see her.'

I wrap the book carefully into an old scarf and gently tuck it into my hand luggage, alongside the copy of *Billy Budd*.

I make one last call before I leave.

Jamie doesn't answer the phone. I leave a message telling him that I am flying back to Boston. Just as I am taking my bags to the door he calls back.

'Hey, you're heading back.'

My heart still leaps at the sound of his voice. 'Yes. My supervisor has passed away.'

'Bummer.'

'Yeah. Bummer. I've been calling you the last two days . . .'

'I know.'

'So why didn't you call me back?' The ghost of my argument with Tanya is making me provoke him.

'You know, I've been busy.'

'We had an agreement that I'd only call if it was something urgent.'

'Okay. I'm sorry. You ring so often when it's not an emergency that I just didn't assume that it was.'

'Do you mind that I call?'

'Well, it wasn't the deal.'

'Yeah, about that. I don't like the deal. I never did. In fact, I think it was your idea, not mine.'

'But you agreed to it.'

'I know. And I'm not sure I should have.'

'Don't do this, Simone. And besides, you're leaving.'

'I noticed you only rang me back when I finally left a message saying that I'm going away again. But I'll be back. And with my supervisor dead now, maybe I'll come back for good.'

There is a silence long enough for me to reflect again on the horror that Professor Young is gone and that I have mentioned it callously, using his death as a way of challenging Jamie.

Finally Jamie replies. 'Don't come back for me, Simone.'

'What do you mean?' I demand.

'You shouldn't factor me into your decisions.'

And suddenly I hear it – what Tanya was saying but I didn't want to hear, what I refused to see.

17

BOSTON, USA

When I finally unlock the door to my apartment I call Tanya.

'Yeah. It's me. Look, no one likes hearing "I told you so",' I say.

'I know.'

'So I'm just going to say that I will never mention Jamie's name again. Ever. And this time I mean it. You were right. I can see that now but I can't talk about it just yet.'

'Sure. I understand. And Simone, I've missed you.'

'Yeah. Me too.'

Professor Louise Baxter's office is lined with shelves neatly stacked with books. Glass ornaments have been placed around the room and they glint when the light hits them. Her room has a feel of unaffected but sophisticated elegance.

'Hello. Take a seat,' she says, walking from behind her desk and motioning to the white leather lounge. She sits in an armchair to my right. 'So you were one of John's students?'

I nod and say what I have been rehearsing since I made the appointment three days ago. 'I hope you don't mind me coming to see you. It's about Professor Young and I know this must be an imposition at a time like this so please forgive me if I seem insensitive. I just didn't know who else to talk to.'

'Of course I don't mind. I realise this is a strange time for many people.' She smiles, sincerely if not warmly.

'I know this sounds odd but a few days after Professor Young passed away a package arrived for me at my home in Australia.'

I take the book gently from my bag. I notice a look of recognition sweep across Professor Baxter's face as I place the book on the table between us. She puts her hand out to touch it, lightly, and then withdraws it.

'It just seems a very generous gift and I thought, given the circumstances, that it might be better if it was kept by someone in his family. His daughter maybe.'

'That's a lovely idea. But if he sent it to you, he did so for a reason. You should keep it. That book did mean a lot to him. It may even have been his most loved possession so he must have wanted you to have it or he wouldn't have gone to all the trouble to get it to you.'

I think of her instinctive touch of the book, the self-conscious withdrawal of her hand. I feel sure I was right about its importance.

'It's just that the package was postmarked the day after he died so he must have put it in the mail the day he . . . well, I just thought that maybe he wasn't thinking straight. I thought it might be more appropriate if his own daughter had it.'

She looks at me as if appraising my earnestness.

'She wouldn't want it.'

'But surely . . .'

'Simone, I am trying to tell you that she wouldn't want it,' she says gently, firmly. 'Without taking anything away from all that was good in John, while he was a great man he was also a complicated man. Complex. Brilliant. But very self-absorbed, selfish. You might not have seen that side of him because, as your supervisor, you would have seen the best of him. With such self-absorption it is very hard to have much left over to give to others and that can make personal relationships also complicated. It is very thoughtful of you to come here and offer but, believe me, trust me, his daughter wouldn't want it.'

'Oh,' I whisper.

Professor Baxter's once soft mouth now seems set firm. I sense I am pushing her too hard so I stop.

'Through all his internal turmoil he obviously made an effort to get that book to you. He must have known you would appreciate it. You should keep it.'

18

After Simone left her office, Louise sat down on the couch. Weariness seeped into her. The book. That damned book. Once she would have coveted it. As soon as Simone had produced it, it brought back memories of the man John had been when she had first met him.

When John had read his poems to her she swelled with the first flushes of dizzy love. Newly married, John's career success, her achievements, and the sheer joy of the girls – how happy she'd been in those days.

And then Lucy's death. She'd watched helplessly as John turned in on himself and destroyed the rest of their world as though Lucy had pulled him into her grave. Louise, even with her own broken heart, tenderly watched over him but his withdrawal made him unreachable. He resisted her every time.

Louise felt helpless against Charmaine's ability to release a spell that she herself had been unable to break.

She had sensed at the time that John was chronically depressed and did not know the words to shake him awake the way Charmaine seemed to. Louise felt she had no choice but to unlock her fingers and let him go. He seemed to have forgotten that she had lost a child too. She could hardly bear her own grief at Lucy's death – a mother's grief – let alone continue with the fruitless, exhausting task of trying to save John as well.

Unlike John, Louise had been able to find great comfort and strength in Jessica and she had tried to soothe her daughter's anger towards him. 'Your father couldn't cope.'

Jessica could never be placated by such entreaties. 'No, Mum. Why do you constantly defend him?'

She understood Jessica's rage, fuelled by John's indifference, his own selfishness. And this resentment only deepened with John's death.

The evening after the funeral, Jessica was sitting on the couch, flicking through television channels with the sound down.

'How are you coping?' Louise asked, sitting beside her.

'Pissed off more than anything else. I was so mad when he left us and I always thought – or hoped – that one day he would see how selfish he was, what a bad father he was to me and apologise for it. At the funeral today I realised he can't do that now. He'll never figure out what he's done, never say "sorry". It's like he's closed a door that I can never open.'

'I think he had a lot of regrets about that.'

'There's no evidence of that. I know that he didn't love me as much as he did Lucy.'

'Parents love their children in different ways. He loved you both but just differently.'

'No. When Lucy died I didn't know what it meant. I even remember thinking that maybe now I'd become Dad's favourite. I know that sounds bad but I was very young. And it shows how deep down inside I always knew I came second.'

Jessica's matter-of-fact tone tugged at Louise's heart. Stripped of her rage, the rawness of Jessica's hurt was gut-wrenching.

'One day, not long after Lucy died, just when I was beginning to understand what her death meant and that she was never coming back, I went to see Dad. He was sitting alone in his study. The room was dark. I called to him and he didn't move, didn't turn to look at me. So I called to him again, waiting for him to look up, to notice me, to take me in his arms, to console me. Still he didn't move or acknowledge that I was there. I called him again, almost pleading for him to say something to me. And he never moved, never even looked up.'

'Oh Jess,' Louise whispered.

'I knew at that moment that I was nothing to him. That not only would I never take Lucy's place but that he would never really love me. Not the way I needed him to love me. Anyway, soon after that he moved in with Charmaine.'

'I know he loved you, Jess. He told me. And you have to remember that your father was a very complicated man,' Louise tried to console her daughter but in the aftermath of Jessica's candid admissions, she felt her reassurances sounded hollow.

Louise was still haunted by that conversation with Jessica. She thought about the forthcoming memorial service. Like the funeral, there would be accolades to celebrate John's achievements, anecdotes about his success, reflections upon his insights and an outpouring of sorrow for the loss of his company, his friendship.

It was only right that the focus be on the good in him, leaving a portrait of an idealistic public intellectual. It was only right that all his failings, all his faults and all the bitterness he would leave behind him should be left unspoken, unacknowledged. It was only right that the bleak look on Jessica's face, the grey resignation, would not be mentioned.

19

Wandering through the University Yard back to the Law School, there is a pinching in my throat. The trickle of tears had begun during the eulogy given by the Dean. Seeing Professor Young through the eyes of others only reminds me of how much I'd admired him, of how much he meant to me. He was more than just my supervisor. He had been a kind of guide, encouraging me to push myself and my ideas in a way that no one else had – apart from my father.

I'm too restless to go home and I find myself instead in the lecture hall where I'd taken my first class with Professor Young. I sit in the same seat I occupied during his classes. I can see him standing at the front. 'I am a zealot among the cynics,' he once exclaimed and laughter rippled through the room.

Since he passed away I've often had a chill of panic when I wonder what his loss means to my work. I'm halfway through my thesis and it's difficult to change supervisors. The task of finding a replacement has been so daunting I don't know where to start. I've thought of just giving up and going home.

Giving up. Just like Professor Young had decided to. I've been going over and over my last conversation with him trying to find a sign, some hint that could explain why he chose to end his life. I've found nothing. Nothing in his book of poems explains it either. And many times I've pondered the mystery of the note he sent with it:

> . . . a loveless world is a dead world . . . there comes an hour when one is weary . . . of devotion to duty, and all one craves for is . . . the warmth and wonder of a loving heart.

It seems to speak of the desolation left by unrequited love, the same theme that runs through Professor Young's book of poetry. The numbness I feel about Professor Young's death is coupled with the despair of realising that Jamie does not care for me, no longer loves me, if he ever did. But Professor Young could not have known that. That's not what he meant by the note.

In the last few days I have re-read *The Plague*, seeking anything that could shed light on the meaning of the phrase. With a title like that, it's pretty obvious that it's a book about death. A plague breaks out in the town of Oran. The gates are shut and it becomes a prison that no one can leave.

Trapped, people have to fight their individual battles against the plague, and also against the suffering and separation that has come with their isolation. People resort to smuggling and start to plan ways to escape so that they can reunite with their loved ones. The plague reaches its worst period in the brutal hot summer months. It kills so many people there is no space left to bury them and the crematorium is working overtime. Everyone suffers from being cut off from the outside world.

The plague ends as suddenly as it began. There is a celebration in the streets, the town gates are opened and families and loved ones return. The book ends with the haunting observation that although the plague bacteria can go into hiding for years, it never disappears for good.

I had discussed the novel with Professor Young, pulling out the themes. In the context of such great suffering, the importance of love to the human spirit becomes clear. The situation created by the plague requires everyone to ask the questions that we should ask ourselves every day. In a crisis that threatens your community, do you flee or do you stay to fight? Do you use the situation for your own advantage or do you volunteer to help? Do you seek others out or do you withdraw within yourself? Do you take action or do you become complacent?

These are the questions that face us all when we are confronted with any great crisis. They provoke us to think about who we are and what our values are. With the possibility of dying so real and so close, every character in the book comes to see themselves and their lives differently. By reflecting on death, they see life more clearly. Professor Young had looked at death and it must have given him more comfort than life. But why?

In re-reading *The Plague* I underlined one phrase that seemed to fit with the one Professor Young had chosen: *If there is one thing one can always yearn for and sometimes attain, it is human love.*

Students for the next class start to come into the lecture hall. When I had started law school back home in Australia I never felt I had the same confidence that other students seemed to naturally possess. Their sense of privilege seemed alien to me. That was, until I found my interest in legal philosophy and legal theory. It gave me a way to explore the bigger ideas that underpin law, a natural match for the passion for social justice that had made me want to study in the first place.

The class is about to start so I leave the lecture hall.

I find myself standing outside the closed office door. 'Professor John Young' is etched on the brass plate. I feel that if I knocked on the door I would hear Professor Young yell, 'Come in.' I put my fingers lightly on the brass doorknob but do not turn it. Nan often tells me that she can hear the voices of the old people who have passed. I used to think she was a bit batty but now I understand what she means.

I close my eyes. I can see him sitting in his chair, half turned away from me, bathed in the sunlight that pours through the window behind him.

'I'm going to miss you, Professor Young,' I whisper. 'I wish you knew what a difference you made to me.'

As I walk home, I can't get my conversation with Professor Baxter out of my mind. The look of recognition on her face when she saw the book, the instinctive touch, has been perturbing me. She told me the book was important to Professor Young. But she was adamant that his daughter would not want it. Was Professor Young's relationship with his daughter strained? She had been there at the memorial service today, sitting beside her mother. She looked sullen, angry and withdrawn. Why wouldn't she be, having just lost her father?

What would happen, I wonder, if my father passed away at this moment? I have struggled lately to reconcile his advocacy for justice with his failings as a person, his unfaithfulness to my mother.

But there's another side to him. The first time I had flown to Boston Mum told me he had stayed at the gate until he could no longer see the plane from the window of the viewing area. He's always provided for me.

He didn't complain about the cost of my going back to study – and at an Ivy League university. He didn't have to support me but he did, uncomplaining, proudly. Despite my scholarships there was a large shortfall and he happily covered that, and he pays my flights home and back whenever I want.

And though it was Professor Young who I had come to talk to about literature and its underlying themes, it was my father who had fostered my love of reading. He would read to me before I went to sleep. He would ask me to bring him the dictionary and I would have to close my eyes and open it to a page. He would then pick a word out, explain its meaning, and I'd have to make a sentence using it. So much of who I am – my politics, my sense of social justice, my identity – comes from him.

'How was the service?' Mum asks when I phone her that night.

'It was lovely. There were lots of people. But . . . I guess I don't really feel that he has gone yet.'

'That's only natural. And in a way he hasn't really. You'll always carry a part of him in your memories.'

'I suppose so. We did have lots of great conversations. Not just about my thesis but all kinds of stuff. Even now I find I remember things he said, little observations about life.'

'Then he'll always be there with you.'

I find her words comforting. 'Can I speak to Dad?'

There is a pause. 'He's not home, sweetheart.' I sense a note of false cheerfulness in her voice.

'Isn't it about six in the morning?'

'He's away. At a conference. Something for work.'

The sight of Dad's hand up the shirt of the young lawyer in his office flashes through my mind and with it comes a white-hot bolt of anger. I also see the ashen face of Professor Young's daughter at the funeral and I can hear Professor Baxter's certainty that she would not want one of her father's most treasured possessions.

'Mum, I'm coming home.'

'Again? Don't you think you should try to get your study back on track?'

'No. I need to sort out some things first.'

20

SYDNEY, AUSTRALIA

'The woman at the reception asked me to stop by on my way to Tony's office. I mean, she said she wanted to see you. I mean, that you wanted to see me.' Darren looked at Rachel beseechingly.

She laughed. 'Yes. Yes, I did. I'd read something after you dropped by last time that made me think of you.'

'You did?'

'Yes. It was this passage, by Fred Maynard.' Rachel searched around the papers on her desk until she found the photocopied page.

'Here it is. Read this. It was taken from a letter he wrote to the New South Wales Premier Jack Lang on 23 August 1927.'

Darren took the paper, hoping that Rachel did not notice the slight shake of his hand as he tried to concentrate on what he was reading.

I wish to make it perfectly clear, on behalf of our people, that we accept no condition of inferiority as compared with the European people. Two distinct civilisations are represented by the respective races. On one hand we have the civilisation of necessity and on the other the civilisation co-incident with a bounteous supply of all the requirements of the human race. That the European people by the arts of war destroyed our more ancient civilisation is freely admitted, and that by their vices and diseases our people have been decimated is also patent, but neither of these facts are evidence of superiority. Quite the contrary is the case . . .

'I think it shows that terms like "invasion" are not new and that the concept of "sovereignty" is not a novel one,' Rachel said.

Darren's first reaction was the gleeful realisation that Rachel Miles had been thinking about him. He suppressed a grin and attempted to look serious.

Tony Harlowe found himself looking forward to his next visit with Darren. He enjoyed reminiscing about the old days, putting his own spin, his own interpretation, on key events. And he enjoyed having Darren for an audience.

'You look flushed. Did you run here?'

At this Darren seemed to colour further. Tony

smiled. This kid, he thought to himself, is still nervous about interviewing me. 'Where're we up to, son?'

Darren flicked through his notebook. 'We were beginning to talk about the legacy of the Tent Embassy.'

'Yes, well, let me emphasise that it's important to see it not just as the catalyst for change but as a symbol of all the changes that occurred around that time. You see, by the time the Tent Embassy was set up, the Aboriginal Legal Service had already been started in Sydney. And the Medical Service too. The people who were around then, who started those services, took that fight, those principles about the need for empowerment, the need to do it ourselves, to the Tent Embassy.'

As Darren made frantic notes, Tony explained that there were over 500 different language groups and tribes with distinct and different needs. 'But three things unite us as Aboriginal people. Our worldviews are similar, we all experience racism because we are Aboriginal and we all have a claim for our rights, especially to land. These are the things we have in common.'

'So the Tent Embassy had a sort of unifying effect, created a national voice,' Darren observed as he jotted in his notebook. After he finished writing, he asked, 'Do you think that when some people today say "land rights didn't work" they are wrong because we didn't really have them?'

Tony explained it to the youngster. Just having schemes through which land can be granted doesn't mean that it is easy to get it back. Governments – both federal and state or territory – fought very hard against the native title or land rights claims of Aboriginal people. And the claim process, he reminded Darren, is time consuming and expensive for Aboriginal communities.

There never had been, in Tony's opinion, the right balance between allowing Aboriginal people to accumulate land as an asset and being able to use it for economic development where the community wants to. Native title gives a right to do things like hunt and fish or perform ceremonies in the way it was done traditionally, but that is hardly going to be a mechanism for Aboriginal people to join the real economy.

'Underlying this is the fact that land rights were never thought of as a panacea. They were seen as only one part of the agenda to overcome Aboriginal disadvantage. Land grants were not going to work to solve poverty while there was no adequate funding for education and proper access to medical services. And the problem is, that despite the view held by many Australians that Aboriginal people are given too much money, that simply isn't the case, and on these key areas – health, housing, education – governments continue to neglect us.'

Darren scribbled furiously to capture every word. So often he had heard the antagonistic slogan that 'land rights haven't worked' and he always knew in his heart that this rhetoric was simplistic, he had just not been able to say why. Tony had articulated exactly what Darren intuitively felt but had never been able to express. 'So land rights were never, on their own, going to compensate for government neglect of basic services?'

Tony nodded. 'Remember with land rights we aren't asking for special treatment. This isn't something for nothing. This is our traditional land. It was taken from us. We were used as slave labour on pastoral properties, were the backbone of the wealth made from farming on our traditional lands. We have no rights over minerals or other natural resources. Australia grows rich from mining and we are left as beggars in our own country. So it's not really land rights. It's land reparation. Land compensation.'

Tony paused to allow Darren to catch up. When his pen slowed, Darren reflected. 'The legal system was very complicit in all of this.'

'Very. That's why you should think about going back to your studies. We need our own people to use the system so that it can be used to protect us, not to always defeat us. I've told you that before.' The words reminded him of the conversations he'd had with Simone when she was in high school, when he was trying to guide her to take the opportunities he never had.

'I know. I've been seriously thinking about it. But I want to get this finished first.' Darren tapped his notebook.

'I was proud when my daughter went to law school. Did you know she's studying overseas now at Harvard, doing her doctorate?'

Darren nodded. Tony had managed to mention it in passing each time they had met.

'Imagine that. And me just a boy from the mission. But that's what we were fighting for back then. To give the next generation the opportunities that we never had. When I look at my daughter, I see the results of that struggle. I guess in the same way your parents must have been proud of you when you were first accepted into university?'

'Well, I suppose my mother was. My father passed away when I was too young to really know him.'

'How does your mother feel about you dropping out? Bet she'd be happy if you went back. I hope you don't mind me saying that. But you seem like a bright young man and, to be honest, I see a bit of myself in you, how I was at your age.'

Darren was too overwhelmed by the comparison with Tony and the sensitive subject of his dropping out of university to answer.

Tony ended the uncomfortable pause. 'Well, maybe they're things to think about before we meet next time.'

Darren nodded. His mother would be happy if he went back to his studies. No doubt about that. But how would his brother react?

21

Darren Brown felt the rhythmic rattle of the train as he travelled home, past Parramatta to the outer western suburb of Mt Druitt. He flicked through his notebook but his thoughts kept coming back to the glow with which Tony Harlowe spoke of his daughter. Raw envy ate at him.

Since dropping out of university he had moved back to his mother's place, the house he'd grown up in. With three of his seven brothers and sisters now out of home, the three-bedroom house was not as crowded as it had been when they were all under one roof. Back then, it was bursting at the seams, rowdy and raucous and there was no privacy.

His mother was on a pension. Money was scarce and, in this environment, resourcefulness was second nature and they made do with little. His father had died in an accident while working on the railway and

Darren had no memory of him. He often wished he had a father – one who would watch him play football and congratulate him after the match, who would talk about him with the same pride that Tony Harlowe spoke about his daughter.

His mother had borne his four youngest siblings with two other men. Both had lived with them sporadically but through drinking or disinterest had never wanted to take on the role of father to Darren. Simon, his eldest brother, was the next best thing. He was charismatic, popular but always getting into trouble. He was very protective of his brothers and sisters but quick to anger if threatened and was easy to goad. He was always getting into fights and the local police came to know him by sight.

It was different in the school holidays when his mother would put him and his siblings on the train and send them to Brewarrina to stay with his grandmother. Baagii, they called her, using the old language. Dozens of cousins and a few uncles would fuss over him, take him fishing, out shooting kangaroo or to the local cricket matches. Baagii's house was crowded with its rooms filled with glassware, photographs and porcelain. The ornate light fittings, dark wallpaper and coffee and tan patterned carpet made the rooms feel even more cramped but everything was always neat. He and his brothers and sisters would sleep in the two rooms, on the couch and lounge room floor, the back verandah and in the old abandoned caravan in the back yard.

These were chaotic times with gangs of children playing games, off to the riverbank or having some kind of adventure. Baagii required them to be home for breakfast and dinner but left them to their own resources in between, knowing the fear of her wrath would be enough to keep everyone on the straight and narrow.

But Darren always sought out her company in the evenings or would play cards with her in the late afternoons. She would tell him stories about her days as a young girl fruit picking with her family and living by the river.

'Tell me the story of how you met my grandfather,' he would ask.

'Again, little Mudhay, my little possum?'

He would nod furiously. He never tired of hearing it.

'Well, he came into town with the boxing tents. He used to work in them and people would pay to fight other men. Your dhaadhaa was the best fighter they had. He arrived in town on the eve of our big dance. Me and my friend Alice had been in Main Street buying some ribbon for our hair. He smiled at us as he walked past and we smiled back. He turned and came back to us and said "Hello, Ladies." But we were shy, brought up right, and we wouldn't tell him our names.

'He asked around and Tommy Hall said, "One is Joan

and the pretty one is Alice." He said to them, "Well, you tell Alice that I want to dance with her at the dance tomorrow night. Tell her I want the first dance and I won't take 'no' for an answer." Well, we got the message and Alice was all giggles and I was right surly as I liked him too, his being so handsome and all.

'But Alice was my friend and I could hold no grudge against her. We spent a lot of time getting ready that night, doing our hair and putting on our dresses. I'd made mine and it was blue with little flowers on it. I know 'cause I still have it packed up in the closet. Well, we get to the dance and there he is, handsome as I remembered him, and he strode right over to us and put his hand out to me and said, "Alice, I believe you owe me this dance." I was so surprised and so happy at the same time. I had to tell him my name was Joan and he said, "Tommy told me the pretty one was Alice and I thought he meant you. You're the prettiest girl I've ever seen." Well, I fell in love with him that night and we were married two months later on my eighteenth birthday.'

Darren loved hearing the way his grandmother laughed as she told the story. His grandfather had died before Darren was born from a heart attack while he was chopping wood. 'He was a strong man with a big heart and we never knew it was a weak one,' his grandmother would say.

There was a photograph of Darren's grandfather that

he loved to look at. Fresh-faced, dark-featured, dark shiny hair, in his boxing shorts, gloved hands pulled to his face.

The racism in Baagii's town had startled him. Being called 'coon', not being served in the shops. Once, when he was walking back with two other boys, a car slowed down and the men in it called them 'dirty little niggers'. 'We're going to hang you from a tree. Here, have a shower, you dirty little niggers,' they had taunted. And then Darren felt the pelts of spit. He had been petrified but, after the men had spat at them, the car roared off.

He knew that the same prejudice existed in the city. The children at his school would call the Aboriginal kids like him 'coon', 'nigger' and 'boong'. He knew that his mother often complained about the way in which she had been treated by the bank, the shopkeepers and the welfare workers. She also said that if Darren's father hadn't been black, they wouldn't have been so slack in making sure he was safe. 'They always give the danger-ous jobs to the blacks,' she would say.

When he started high school, the form master, Mr Hestelowe, seemed to take an interest in him. One day towards the end of his first year he had taken Darren aside. 'Why don't you stick to your studies?' he asked. 'You get good marks when you apply yourself.'

Darren shrugged.

'You never do your homework.'

'I find it hard, sir.'

'You need to apply yourself.'

Darren didn't say that the house was overcrowded, there was no space for him to do homework and it was noisy. The younger kids always needed attention and Simon always had some scheme or adventure.

'You could stay back at school and do it.'

'Aw, then all my mates would laugh at me.'

'Not cool, eh?'

Darren shook his head.

The next day, in assembly, Mr Hestelowe had called him out. 'Darren Brown, report to my office at the end of the day. You're on detention this afternoon.'

Darren was fuming. He'd done nothing wrong and there was Mr Hestelowe just yesterday acting as though he was concerned about him, but today he was falsely accusing him, making a fool of him in front of the whole school. He came to the office, full of rage, when the final bell rang.

'Get your books out and do your homework.'

Darren would stay back after school and do his homework under the pretence he was in trouble. His marks improved.

'I noticed in your English essay you wrote about the way your mother was treated in the store when it was assumed that she was a shoplifter because she was black,' he once said.

'It's all racist and people get away with it.'

'It is illegal to discriminate against people on the basis of their race when you are buying goods in a store. There are laws against it.'

'Well why don't they work? We cop it all the time.'

'It's only in some circumstances and you have to bring a case,' Mr Hestelowe explained.

'Like a court case? We can bring a case?'

'Well, you usually need a lawyer to help.'

'A lawyer. Aren't they expensive?'

'They are. But I guess if you were a lawyer you wouldn't need to pay one.'

Since then Darren would dream about it, imagine he was in court, just like it was on television. He would lay the story out to the judge and use his powers of persuasion.

But Darren didn't go to university. He left school and started packing for the local supermarket. Mr Hestelowe had encouraged him to apply for university but none of his friends had gone and his brother Simon had said it was for wankers.

Six months later, his cousin, who had epilepsy, had a fit on a train station on his way home from work. The train staff took him to the hospital. The nurse on duty looked at his dark skin and concluded that he was drunk. The police came and took him to the lock-up and overnight he died in custody.

Darren's anger at the injustice of what had happened sparked his interest in going back to study. He went up to the school and spoke to Mr Hestelowe who helped him to apply for special admission to university. He did a bridging course, and while that went well enough, once he had started the uni course found it was much harder. There was further disruption in the house when his mother fell ill and two of his sisters – sixteen and seventeen – both got themselves pregnant within three months of each other. His friends and Simon had viewed him with suspicion. 'You becoming an uptown nigger?' his brother would taunt.

Darren took on extra shifts to help his mother meet her bills and towards the end of the year he dropped out of uni before he was formally marked as having failed his courses. 'Don't worry,' Simon would console, 'you'll be like us again now. We had nothing in common when you were doing that uni stuff. Not because we aren't proud of you. But we just don't understand it. Going to prison, we can relate to that.'

Not long after that, Baagii died and it felt as though his world had fallen apart. Darren became restless and angry, as though a ball of frustration had knotted inside him. When some of his friends mentioned a car trip to Canberra to join a protest about changes to the native title legislation, he jumped at the chance. He'd always liked hearing Aboriginal leaders speak. Tony Harlowe, Gary Foley, Michael Mansell – they had all come to speak at the university when he had been there and each had spoken in a way that he understood.

So he joined his friends to go for a weekend and found, at the Tent Embassy, a language of politics and a worldview that captured his anger, frustration and his desire for a better life for people like his mother. He found himself there for a week, then two, and then signed on as part of the lobby to get the Tent Embassy status on the National Trust as a significant historical site.

It had been a good distraction from the dislocation and the despondency he had felt when coming to terms with the loss of his grandmother. Baagii had believed in the spirits. 'Don't go near the river at night,' she would warn. 'There are spirits there. They eat little birralii like you. And if you go too far out of the town at night, away from the lights, they can get you then too. Not all spirits are bad though. The old people look over you, and the young ones who die too young have the most sorrow. They are the most restless. I always believed in ghosts but I didn't start to hear them until after your dhaadhaa passed away. I started to hear them then. And you might think that is funny but I started to get messages from time to time from the dead to pass on to the living.'

'Will you come and talk to me after you die, Baagii?'

She would laugh in her rich throaty way. 'I hope that won't be for a while yet, Mudhay.' When she stopped laughing she would say, 'When you hear the rain on the roof, that will be me, coming back to watch over you.'

Even now he loved the sound of heavy rain. He would find somewhere to pretend he was asleep – in a crowded house you had to learn how to escape the noise by simply closing your eyes – and would listen to the rain and try to work out what Baagii was telling him.

As the train pulled into the station, Darren thought of Rachel. Since that first time he'd seen her, she'd been on his mind. It must be the same feeling that his grandfather felt when he first saw his grandmother – that here was the most beautiful girl he had ever seen, soft and pretty, but so refined. She spoke so nicely, lady-like. And was smart, educated. He'd not have thought to hope if she hadn't found the snippet from Maynard for him. That she had remembered their brief conversation when he had delivered some phone messages and thought of him at least once again when she had seen the letter, gave him some cause to think he may have a chance with her.

His next meeting, and probably the last, with Tony Harlowe, would be in two weeks. He had to think of a way, between now and then, to ask Rachel out.

22

Tony had back-to-back meetings so it wasn't until the end of the day that he had a chance to reflect on his interview with Darren. Thinking about the political struggle over the years brought him to think of Simone. She was his greatest achievement. And yet, his pride was tightly entwined with sadness at the way their closeness now stretched into such distance.

Tony Harlowe's third rule for survival was: always know who you are dealing with. It had served him well to find out all he could about not just his enemies but his allies and friends. Knowing their nature, what motivated them, their strengths and weaknesses had armed him in his public battles. It had served him well in his private ones as well, with the sole exception of Simone. His daughter was the one person he didn't know how to deal with, didn't know how to read.

She hadn't spoken to him about what she had seen when she had walked into the office that day but had eyed him derisively. He was too ashamed to talk to her about it. What the scene revealed hung heavily between them. He knew that she knew but how could he explain? What did he possibly have to say for himself? The only thing that he would want Simone to understand was that Rachel was no throw-away woman, no ill-considered fling. However disposable his indiscretions had been in the past, Rachel was different.

Just as he was thinking of her, Rachel knocked at the door. His heart swelled when he saw her.

'Hi,' she said, 'Ready to go?'

'Give me fifteen minutes. I'll come to your office.'

'Sure,' Rachel smiled and left.

He put his head in his hands. He was going to have to do something soon. He couldn't keep going like this. He longed for Rachel all the time. As soon as he left her, he wanted to see her again. She crept into his thoughts every waking moment, distracting him. And when he was with her, what contentment he felt. He loved talking to her about legal matters, the way she questioned him about his work, about the community politics. He loved the way she felt – her skin so soft and smelling like flowers and honey. She was beautiful when naked, her body a confluence of curves and leanness. She was, he thought, the most perfect thing he had ever seen.

And so the idea that he needed to be with her, to make a life with her, had occupied his thoughts more and more over the last few weeks. He had even decided that he would give Beth Ann the house and half of the superannuation. He'd be generous. After all, Beth Ann had been there from the start and had done nothing wrong; she was the innocent party in all of this. He'd promised he would always look after her, especially when she had wanted to go to university or work full-time. No, he had always said firmly, I'll take care of you. And he wasn't going to go back on his word now.

He loved Beth Ann, always would. She had been a good wife, a perfect mother. None of this turn of events, this fate, was her fault. But neither was it his. He would see her looked after but he also needed to travel this other path. He would sell the investment property and begin his new life with Rachel with the proceeds. His fiftieth birthday might be looming but Rachel gave him the energy to feel that life was starting over.

Tony's musings were interrupted by the shrill ring of the phone. 'I've got your mother on the line,' announced Carol Turner.

'Tell her I'm busy, that I'm in a meeting.'

'I can't. She's deaf, remember, or as good as. Besides, you're not in a meeting and it's disrespectful to lie to our Elders.'

'You're supposed to be my assistant and look out for me.'

'Lying to your mother isn't in my job description. I'm putting her through and you can sort it out. I'm heading off. Goodnight.'

Tony heard the click of the connection.

'Anthony, is that you?'

'Yes, Mum.'

'What?'

'Yes, it's me,' he said louder.

'Good. Now listen. I've just heard from Julia Murray that Pam Briggs's son Matthew was killed last weekend. Car accident. Third fatal one at Wellington. All young people too. The council was supposed to do something about the signs but never did.

'I was also up at the local Land Council last night. We've got elections coming up and they want me to stand. I told 'em I wasn't going to if it meant that I'd have to put up with that Tom Riley as CEO. He's a good-for-nothing. Remember when he took over the health service out here and almost ran it into the ground? The good Lord gave me plenty of patience but not that much. I told Jimmy when he was voted Chair last year not to put him on but, you know Jimmy, can't be told anything. Always thinks he knows what's best.'

'Mum, I've got to go, I've got a meeting.'

'What?'

'A meeting. I've got a meeting.'

'I know. That's what I'm talking about. The Land Council meeting. I swear by the good Lord, if ever you listened to me properly I'd be so surprised I'd fall off my chair. So anyway, everyone was there and we have been asked by the Shire to sign an agreement and I said we shouldn't unless it included being able to raise our flag on the council building and at the school. That's not asking for much. Just a little recognition.'

Tony sighed. He tried again, this time speaking louder. 'Mum, I've got to go.'

'All right. No need to shout.'

That, thought Tony as he hung up the phone, was going to be another difficult conversation. 'You can get an appetite while you are out but always eat at home,' his mother would say. She was a strong believer in marriage and in fidelity. She was also very fond of Beth Ann. He couldn't bear to think about how his mother would react to Rachel.

But it was Beth Ann whose reaction was going to be the hardest for him to bear. He had rehearsed his speech about how he felt they had grown apart and that he needed a change. That he wouldn't be who he was without her but that he needed some time on his own. He would always love her and was hoping they could part as friends. Surprisingly, he found himself with a growing tenderness for Beth Ann now that he'd decided to leave her.

He'd decided that he would separate from her without disclosing his relationship with Rachel. Just so he wouldn't hurt her further. After a period of time, he and Rachel could then make their relationship public. And in the meantime, he relished the idea of new rituals and routines – Saturday morning reading the papers, Sunday brunch, late afternoon movies. He would always acknowledge that he would not be who he was if it hadn't been for Beth Ann's support but with Rachel he could see the promise of a new era. As a team, with his experience and her education, they would be a formidable force.

He'd also rehearsed how he would tell Rachel that he was leaving his wife for her. He'd not said it yet, waiting to be sure, not wanting to get her hopes up until he was certain he would be able to finally break with Beth Ann. But when he imagined letting Rachel know that his love for her was so profound, that he had decided to forsake the life he had to build a new one with her, he imagined her surprise and her acute happiness. And the thought of her reaction gave him strength to execute what would be the most difficult of all – the discussion he had to have with Beth Ann.

But not tonight. Tonight he would continue with the lies.

He rang Beth Ann and was relieved when he got the answering machine. 'Hi, love. Just ringing to let you know that I have a late work meeting. Should be there at about nine. I'll have dinner out so don't worry about me.'

23

One week ago, everything had changed for Beth Ann. Some people's lives would be altered by cataclysmic events – fatal car accidents, house fires, train wrecks, suicides. Hers altered with a phone call; with a simple question and a casual, seemingly innocent answer.

Tony had gone to Lightning Ridge for a meeting and she'd wanted to tell him that Simone had called and was coming home. She persistently rang his mobile but it kept going straight to voicemail. Beth Ann knew that sometimes in these country areas far from the city mobile reception wasn't very good.

She could picture the small motel Tony was staying in – its teal doors, the sandy brick walls, yellowed laminated floors, the floral bedspreads and curtains. These country town motels seemed all cut from the same mould.

She'd rung the main switch and asked for Tony Harlowe's room.

'I'm sorry, Mr and Mrs Harlowe aren't answering,' the woman on the other end replied.

'This *is* Mrs Harlowe,' Beth Ann had said in a slow, determined voice.

The woman on the line had faltered. 'Oh.'

Beth Ann could imagine her too. Short, with an abundant, fleshy body, a face hardened from work but soft eyes.

'Yes. "Oh", indeed.'

Beth Ann hung up. She sat there by the phone feeling as though her insides had been ripped out. She felt hollow.

'Mrs Tony Harlowe' was ringing in her ears. She spent the next few hours not only reeling from the betrayal but also wondering when it was that she stopped feeling like Beth Ann Gibson.

Even though she had felt Tony's betrayal before, this time it was different. She knew it as she looked in the bathroom mirror, stared at her face. The same face she'd always had but now ripened with lines and, in this light, looking tired, drained. It wasn't just the realisation that after thirty years together, twenty-nine years of marriage and twenty-six years of being parents, that Tony Harlowe was never going to change. This time it was something more.

This time, Tony was being more open about his infidelity, less discreet. And this time, while some of her emotions were so familiar – the humiliation, the knotted rage, feeling small and insignificant – she felt different too. Amidst her inner tumult was not resignation but the seeds of weariness.

All those years ago when she arrived in Canberra there was a mass of tents and tarpaulins, even umbrellas. People – black and white – had come from all over. While there was a group of Aboriginal people who had made up a kind of cabinet – making the decisions, deciding the strategies – she, like many others, was there to simply show that she too thought this fight was important.

There she had met Tony. But she had met his friend Arthur Randall first, timidly sitting on the edge of a throng of people. When she shyly joined them he turned to her and smiled. They got talking and didn't stop for almost three hours. She felt flushed, knowing it was more than just the Canberra heat. He shared dinner with her from the communal pots and pans, the food that people from around Canberra had dropped off for them, and they stayed talking around one of the camp fires. She told him about Murray Simms. He told her about life on the mission.

She went to bed that night thinking about Arthur, his thoughtful dark eyes, his mellow voice. And the next morning he had introduced her to Tony Harlowe. Tony was in the thick of what was going on, in with the people who were the heart of the protest. Arthur had taken her to one of the meetings of the inner sanctum and, as she sat silently on the outside of the circle, she could feel Tony's eyes upon her. He flashed her a smile and she felt herself blush. He was handsome, confident.

The more attention Tony paid her, the more Arthur seemed to recede into the background. And while she sought out Arthur for his company and conversation, he started to avoid her, found reasons not to sit with her, became elusive. All the time, Tony demanded more and more of her.

It was the fact that she still had feelings for Arthur that made her refuse Tony's first offer of marriage. They were both so young. She had only known him for a few weeks; she hadn't taken him seriously. Tony was so brash but Arthur, quieter, less dazzling, seemed more solid, more reliable.

Tony followed her to Sydney when she started her studies and asked her again. She refused the second time because she was not sure that she was ready to make such a commitment, ready to give up her only chance to see what she could make of her own life. But he was persistent. The third time he proposed he was so earnest. He made many promises but the thing that made her say 'yes', despite her fears and misgivings, was that over the months she had grown to love Tony. That Christmas, she left her studies and in the new year became Mrs Tony Harlowe.

And being Mrs Tony Harlowe had become a full-time job. Much like the first time she met him, she sat quietly on the edge of his circle and let him take the stage. She believed in his work and always knew how important it was. It was a role that only he could perform and she, as a white person, was limited to the supporting role. She wanted to be out of the spotlight. She was proud of what he had achieved. And she felt, even though she had never pushed her way to centre stage, that she had assisted Tony to play an important role. It was, at its heart, an Aboriginal fight but it was something everyone, Beth Ann felt, had a part to play in fixing.

She happily became a full-time wife and then, three years later when Simone arrived, a mother. She had loved that, nurturing a child. She had never been able to conceive a second – though she had wanted to at first. She had planned to have a large family but while she had been trying – unsuccessfully – to conceive again she had begun to have doubts about Tony. Not as a father, but as a husband.

Over time, she lost regular contact with her family. Tony had always resisted visiting them, finding some excuse not to go. She would write to her sisters and call at Christmas but their lives had taken different directions. Her parents passed away – her father from colon cancer and her mother of a heart attack – dead at the table, two empty bottles of vodka beside her.

Tony was almost as estranged from his family as she eventually became from hers. He would make the odd reference to his childhood, tell the occasional story about it but Beth Ann never could get him to explain why he refused to go back to the place where he grew up. In all the time she had known him he had gone there only once, not long after their wedding. It was for his sister Emily's funeral. Tony had been grief-stricken, crushed. He could barely speak about his sister's death – had scarcely mentioned her in the years since – but the impact when he had first heard the news was visible. He had been firm about going to the funeral on his own. He had timed his arrival to coincide with the beginning of the service and left as soon as the wake started.

His mother, Frances, came to visit from time to time, not so often now she was older, but she still phoned regularly. Beth Ann had a good rapport with her, loved her spirit and her stories but, like her son, she never spoke of Emily, or why her son would never go home and why she never insisted that he did.

Beth Ann never minded that she had little support to raise Simone. In fact, she loved being alone with her daughter. But as Simone grew older, she seemed to become closer to her father and adored him in a way that Beth Ann could never compete with. Not that Beth Ann was too bothered; she understood the attractions of Tony Harlowe. She did, however, miss the closeness of the relationship she had with her daughter when Simone was very young.

When Simone was about five, Beth Ann volunteered to teach literacy in the prison as she found it hard to fill her day. Tony had thundered his disapproval at first but she had persevered and even enlisted a few others to exert some influence and gently put pressure on him. Years later, she had felt Simone's departure from the house keenly. Simone's study overseas had been hard to bear for Beth Ann who, even though she was so proud of her daughter's achievements, missed her. Once, Simone had been enough to distract her from her unhappiness with Tony. Now she was gone, the emptiness became impossible to avoid.

Something hard had grown within her, setting even more solidly as she heard the answering machine two nights ago.

Hi love. Just ringing to let you know that I have a late work meeting. Should be there at about nine. I'll have dinner out so don't worry about me.

The lies. The easy slip of lies.

24

I love it when someone is at the airport to pick me up, especially after a long flight. It is a comforting thought to know that you have arrived in a place where you have someone who cares about you.

'Hello, sweetheart.' Mum hugs me as I walk through the waiting throng and into her arms. I'm surprised when she starts to cry.

'Are you all right?'

'Yes. Yes. Of course. Of course I am. I am just so pleased to see you.'

'I was home only two weeks ago.'

'Yes, I know. But I'm your mother. Two weeks is a long time.'

I've been away for almost a year before this spate of quick visits and never got tears before but I let it pass.

'How was the trip?' Mum asks after we've packed my bags in the back seat of her car and begun the journey home. I can see she is still teary – those telltale red rims around her eyes.

'Fine. I read a book on the plane. *Billy Budd*. It was Professor Young's favourite. He talked about it all the time.'

'That's a nice way to remember him. Does his favourite book reveal anything?'

'Do you know the book?'

'I've heard of it but I've never read it.'

I tell Mum the basic storyline. The book is set in the late 1790s and tells the story of a sailor in the Royal Navy, Billy Budd. He's an orphaned, illegitimate child but innocent and open, a little naive but likeable, popular with everyone. For some reason, probably jealousy and false gossip from a crew mate, he arouses the antagonism of the ship's Master-at-Arms, John Claggart, who falsely accuses Billy of conspiracy to mutiny.

Claggart brings his charges to Captain Vere who summons them both to his cabin. Claggart makes his false charges but Billy is unable to defend himself. He has a speech impediment and isn't articulate, can't argue. He gets so frustrated about not being able to properly express himself and counter the charges that he lashes out involuntarily at Claggart, killing him with a single blow.

Captain Vere convenes a court martial. At his insistence, they convict Billy; Vere argues that any appearance of weakness in the officers and failure to enforce discipline could stir the waters of mutiny throughout the British fleet. Billy is condemned to be hanged from the ship's yardarm.

'That's not a very cheery story. Not a very happy ending,' Mum says when I have finished.

'I know. When I discussed it with Professor Young he said that Captain Vere deliberately distorted the law to bring about Billy's death. The story shows how when we apply the law in a seemingly fair but narrow way, without considering the idea of justice more broadly, it can create a huge wrong. That's why Professor Young liked the book, I think. He was always interested in whether laws were applied fairly or whether they were applied in a way that might have *seemed* fair but actually caused great injustice. It was what he was known for. All the books he was most famous for were about that.'

'It sounds like Professor Young was a very fine man. A man with great principles.'

'He was. And I always found him so. You know how I admired him, even worshipped him really. And part of that was because he did have a sincere interest in justice and fairness, making sure that people were treated properly by the law and were not victims of its manipulation. But . . .'

'But what?' Mum asks, glancing sideways at me as she drives.

I'm thinking about my encounter with Professor Baxter.

'But I don't think it reveals as much about him as the fact that I don't think his daughter liked him very much.'

'Goodness, whatever gave you that idea?'

We have arrived in the driveway. 'Make me a cup of tea, Mum, and I'll tell you all about it.'

By the time we finish the tea I have relayed the details of the unsettling conversation. Professor Young's book sits on the table between us, like a court exhibit.

'She was so sure, Mum, so sure that his own daughter wouldn't want it. She told me the book was very important to him. She said it was perhaps his most valued possession. Yet she was so adamant about not taking it.'

Mum pours me another cup of tea. I run my fingers across the leather of the books spine.

'Well, I guess you can never know the whole story of what happened in his family.'

'I guess. I saw his daughter at the memorial service. She looked, I don't know, so angry. Her father was dead and she had all this rage. And I thought, I never want to feel that way about Dad.'

'Of course not, Simone. Why would you? Your father loves you.'

I smile back at her but it is false.

I don't doubt my father loves me. The problem is that since I saw him in that embrace I have not been able to get it out of my mind. And the more I dwell on it, the more I detest him. And I'm sure that is why the image of Professor Young's daughter haunts me and why my encounter with Professor Baxter keeps coming to mind. I can see myself feeling like that, small and hard with my hate like a little nut. And if Dad died this minute I may have no way of letting it go.

I clearly can't talk to Mum about why I am so angry at Dad. I could never hurt her that way.

There is only one person who I can have that conversation with and that is Patricia Tyndale.

25

When I was younger and I wanted to know something, Dad would say, 'Why don't you ring Patricia and ask her.'

Even though she was a regular in our house, close with both my parents and with Tanya's as well, the idea of speaking to her filled me with such fear that I would mumble, 'It's all right. I'll work it out for myself. It's not that important.'

Patricia was always tough and forthright and it took a while for me to realise that she was also generous, kind. As I grew older I appreciated her qualities, along with the wisdom of her life experience. Even now I still feel nervous with her, a hangover from my childhood, but I always cherish the time I spend in her company. I like hearing her speak – about 'the old days', community politics, what I should be doing with my life. There are always long pauses in our conversation and she has periods of being so quiet that sometimes I wonder if she remembers that I am present.

'The silences are just as important as the words,' Nan had said to me once but it is an insight that does not sit well with my impatience. I like looking at Patricia in those long pauses. She has the kind of timeless beauty that only gets richer with age, is not spoiled by lines.

'How's that fellow of yours?' she asks as we sit down.

'Over,' I say, fidgeting. 'Didn't really last with me going overseas and all.' Once speaking about Jamie would have me lamenting and talking about how wonderful he was but our last phone conversation has killed off my delusions and my last trip to the States has completely pushed him out of my mind.

Patricia offers me a cigarette. I smile at her but shake my head. She shrugs, taking one from the packet for herself. 'Well, nicotine always works for me.' She clicks her lighter and winks at me as she takes a deep drag. 'It's good this coming and going you've taken to of late. I'm doing very nicely with the duty free.' She smiles her wry smile. 'So what brings you around?'

'Something I saw.'

She is dragging on her cigarette but she raises an eyebrow.

'I surprised Dad at the office a couple of weeks back and . . . well . . . I caught him in an embrace with one of the young lawyers there. Rachel Miles.'

'What did your father do?'

'I walked out before he could say anything but he had guilt plastered all over his face. And his hand was up her shirt.'

She holds my gaze and I try to read her. I've never been able to work out what she's thinking but I know I don't see surprise on her face.

'Have you said anything to him since?'

'I can't. I keep avoiding him. I couldn't bear to hear him try to explain himself or justify it and I just don't know what to say to him. I'm so furious about it, with him. I don't know why he's doing this to Mum. And I don't know why he's doing it to me. And now, every time he prattles on about land rights and human rights and any other kind of rights I think, well, what about acting like a good person? Why be yammering on about how the world needs to be just and fair when you behave like such a bastard? How can he be so self-righteous when he has no morals?'

I pause. Patricia is still looking at me and it is a long moment before she answers.

'Just because someone is a bastard doesn't mean they don't have rights, you know. Human rights are not just there for people who are good. They are there for everyone. Including those with flaws like your father.'

'Yeah, I know. I know. If it was a matter of being perfect to deserve them, none of us would be entitled to them,' I reply grimly.

There is more silence as she inhales her cigarette and then watches as the smoke dissipates into the air as she exhales. She doesn't speak again until she determinedly stubs out the cigarette.

'I want to show you something,' she announces.

She rises from her chair and leaves the room, re-emerging some time later armed with a scrapbook. She drops it in front of me and nods. I start to thumb through it. It is full of clippings, the paper yellowed and fragile with age. There are stories about my father – profiles of him, stories about speeches he has given, legal cases of importance that the legal service had won.

'I have kept these over the years. Helps with my memory for when I write my memoirs one day.'

'That will be some book.'

'Indeed. But I'll have to write them when some of these people are dead. Just so I can tell the whole truth and nothing but the truth. I'll call them *Betraying Bastards I Have Known*.' She sniffs as she reaches for her cigarette packet again.

'And what about Dad?'

Patricia stops pulling the cigarette from the packet, lost in thought. She looks out her apartment windows to the train lines and streets below. It seems like several minutes before she turns to me. 'I think your father was always afraid of me. I don't know why, but I seem to have that effect on men.' She finally pulls the cigarette out and lights it. 'I've known him for a long time. I know most of his secrets so he can't hide much from me.'

'Was he always a womaniser?'

'There were always plenty of women who were attracted to your father. You might find this hard to believe because you're his daughter but women were very drawn to him.'

'Oh, I know that. And I can see why. But the thing is, why does he have to act on it? That's the part that gets me. Where's his moral compass?'

'You're very judgmental.'

'He's my father. I should have an opinion.'

'Go to the back page of that scrapbook.'

I dutifully turn and there is an interview with my father from the *Koori Mail*, in a question and answer style.

'Read that,' Patricia orders.

It asks questions like 'where are you from?' and 'what is your favourite meal?', 'what is your favourite song?' and 'what is your favourite movie?'. Then there is the question: 'How would you spend the last night of your life?' He has answered: I would stay up all night with my daughter Simone, talking and laughing.

'I don't doubt he loves me. That's not the point. What about Mum?'

'Your father is a complicated man.'

'So everyone tells me.'

Patricia ignores me. There is a stoniness creeping into her voice when she continues.

'You know what I think you should do? I think you should go home and visit your grandmother. We're Aboriginal people. When something goes wrong or we have a problem that needs working out, we go home, back to our country. It's what we do, where we are strongest. That's why we ask "Where are you from?" when we meet someone, not "What do you do?" You should go home and visit your grandmother.'

26

'I always know it's you if the phone rings this late at night.'

'Well, you're about the only person who I can rely on to help me get to sleep,' Patricia sighed.

Arthur laughed. 'That doesn't sound like a compliment.'

'You know what I mean.'

'So you're having another restless night?'

'I was lying in bed but just couldn't sleep. I'm out on the balcony, enjoying a smoke and watching the streets below. They're as restless as I feel.'

'What's on your mind?'

'I don't know. Tony's daughter was here today. She's as angry with her father as she was when you saw her at Tanya's. That deep, deep anger that gets richer with time. I tried to show her how much he loved her. I had a clipping in a scrapbook. But opening it was like unlocking a box of memories.'

'Well, you've been fighting the good fight for a long time now. Longer than it would be polite to mention.'

'You've been there as long as I have,' Patricia replied.

'True. But you've put your heart into it. And I had Sarah and the girls to lift me up. You've never had that.'

'Maybe that's why they call it a political *struggle*. It always feels like a fight.'

'And you've paid a high price for it.'

'I have. I've felt myself harden over the years. I don't know how to compromise.'

'You might be tough on the outside but I know you, my girl, and there is a very big heart beating in there.'

'It feels like that soft part gets smaller and smaller. But I've seen those people – and you know the ones I mean – who have so much bitterness in them that there is no softness left. I worry I will become one of them, one of those people with nothing but hardness.'

'You have me.'

Patricia smiled. 'Yes. I have you. It's a good friend who lets you ring at all hours of the night understanding that you are an insomniac.'

'And a not very cheery one,' Arthur teased.

Patricia put the phone back in the receiver and lit another cigarette. Sometimes speaking with Arthur would soothe her and she would be able to sleep. Other times – and tonight was one of them – she would feel as restless as before she rang.

It had been the talk with Simone and the flood of memories that was haunting her. Even after all these years, she could remember every detail of that time when she had first met Tony. She had watched so intently, playing every scene over and over in her mind, and interpreting every detail.

It was out of character for her to sit quietly by, just watching. While she was outspoken when it came to politics, she found herself mute when it came to her heart. And often, on these nights when she could not sleep, she would think about all the 'what ifs', rehearsing what she wished she had said.

Tony was brash even then, confident, but she had always seen beyond that. She sensed he had secrets, that there was much more to him than others knew. And that first time he smiled at her had burnt deep into her memory – the sideways glance, glinting eyes and that dark curl across his forehead. No one would have guessed how much it had melted her heart.

In the throng of the discussions, the heated debates about what to do next, the detailed planning of what to write, what to say and who should do what, Patricia found herself timid when Tony was around. Yet when he flirted with her, she succumbed. Late that night, that fateful night, amid the smell of burning wood and people sweating, the sounds of laughter and guitars twanging, Tony sat down close to her, so close she thought he would feel her heart beating. And that night, under the tents, in the midst of history in the making he kissed her, placed his hands on her body. She could feel her skin respond to his.

And just as Patricia never forgot that night, she remembered the next morning just as clearly. She felt she was shining from within and was convinced that everyone would know just by looking at her. She glowed. He looked sheepish.

But later that same day, the very day that Patricia thought was the beginning, it all ended. Patricia didn't notice Beth Ann when she first arrived. She was sitting at the back of a group assembled in one of the main tents. Patricia had been watching Tony, following his every move, and saw that his eyes kept being drawn towards the woman who was sitting beside Arthur. Patricia watched as Tony betrayed both her and his best friend to get his heart's desire.

By that time, things had culminated with the protest too. Everyone knew the police were poised to move so they put the women and children in the frontline. They will not arrest the women, everyone had said. There were arguments that night about what to do but Patricia, so burning with rage about Tony and his easy dismissal, was happy to put herself on the line, to put her slender body in front.

She had linked arms with the others, shouted 'Land Rights Now' and sang 'We Shall Not Be Moved.' There were hundreds of people standing by,

watching – tourists with their cameras, public servants in their suits. It was mid-morning when the police
moved in. Their fists smashed against Patricia's flesh
and she ended up in the hospital.

When she was released, she returned to the Embassy.
By then Tony had left, following Beth Ann to Sydney.

Patricia had never spoken about that night to Tony.
She was glad of the silence, fearing that any attempt to
laugh off as a joke a memory she held so dearly would
cheapen it. A part of her hoped Tony's romance with
Beth Ann wouldn't last but deep down she knew it
would, could see it in Tony's face that he loved Beth
Ann with the same depth that Patricia loved him.

Patricia kept the scrapbook of him. Not of everyone,
as she had pretended to Simone. She didn't need help
to keep her memories, but the clippings represented a
part of him that she could have.

Patricia returned to her bedroom. She slipped
between the sheets and turned the bedside light off.
She could picture the embrace that haunted Simone.
She too had heard the rumours over the years, caught
the whispers and winks, and she was always curious
whether Beth Ann knew. She wondered, couldn't help
herself, that if Tony had chosen her, how she would
have coped with his infidelity.

Still, whatever Tony's faults, she loved him. Always
had. Never wavered. Staring at the ceiling, Patricia
waited for sleep to come. She wondered how long it

would take Simone to realise that to love someone despite their faults, to love the whole person, good and bad, is to truly love them.

27

'I think this might be the last time,' Darren said as he settled into his seat.

'We'd better make it a good one then,' Tony replied with a grin.

Darren grinned back and opened his notebook at the next blank page. 'We've spoken about the history of activism by Aboriginal people in Australia that provided the intellectual ground for the Tent Embassy, but what were the international influences?'

'At the Embassy we used the language of rights. We didn't make them up. They came from international law, from the documents produced by the United Nations. The concept of human rights was the intellectual driving forces of the Magna Carta and the American and French revolutions. Thomas Paine, Benjamin Franklin and Thomas Jefferson were talking about universal human rights long before we were.'

Tony continued, explaining how claims to human rights were more than just the chattering of the elite. They concerned important aspects of the day-to-day lives of people who were disempowered – the right to equality, the right to a fair wage, the right to make decisions. He dismissed the idea that you have either a rights agenda or practical outcomes.

'Take the right to be free from racial discrimination. It is a universal human right, protected by several of the key international human rights instruments and there is even one especially dedicated to preventing it – the Convention to Eliminate all forms of Racial Discrimination. We have adopted that convention into Australian law through the federal Racial Discrimination Act and it provides us with a mechanism to make a complaint about racial discrimination to the Human Rights Commission. So there is a tangible remedy for it now. People can actually make a complaint if they feel that they have been unfairly treated.'

Darren nodded as he wrote and Tony paused to allow him to catch up. He looked at the familiar furrow in Darren's forehead, the one that made him appear intense but thoughtful. His black shiny hair was pulled back into a ponytail but his slight sideburns formed small curls. When Darren seemed to have caught up, Tony continued.

'Anti-discrimination laws have led to profound changes. Even though there may be few landmark cases and the discrimination is only prohibited in certain circumstances, look at the impact of those laws. Pretty much every workplace now has policies in place that prevent racial discrimination in employment. They have policies to prohibit sexual harassment in the workplace. Companies run training and information sessions for employees about what discrimination is and to emphasise that it needs to be avoided. If you compared the way the workforce was before these laws with how it operates now, you would begin to understand the important impact that legislating a right can have on the community.'

When Tony paused, Darren took the opportunity to ask a question. 'You were saying last time that land rights were never considered to be a panacea. How did you think they would assist in delivering social justice?'

'You have to remember that getting land rights doesn't mean the government is no longer responsible for ensuring that our communities have adequate housing, health and education facilities. Other Australians have assets and that doesn't mean that the government is no longer responsible for providing them with the necessities. The statistics show that federal and state governments continue to underfund on all of these areas for Aboriginal people, even though we have the lowest levels of income and education, the poorest levels of health and the worst standards of housing. Having land rights will only do so much when you don't have education, health and housing.'

Tony went on to explain that even if the government provided these basic necessities at appropriate levels, it didn't mean that the claim for land compensation and land rights was no longer legitimate.

When Tony finally paused, Darren closed his book. 'Thank you so much. I can't thank you enough for all your help. It's been an honour just to listen to you speak. I'll send the transcripts of all our discussions through to you when I have typed these up, just to make sure you are happy with everything.'

'Well, the pleasure has been mine. I've certainly relived some old memories doing these interviews.' Tony stood and stretched his arms and legs. 'I'll walk you out.'

'It's okay. I know the way.'

'I have to go down to the front anyway.'

Darren gave a tight smile. He had been planning to stop by at Rachel Miles's office before he left. Her door had been closed when he had arrived. He was just as disappointed when he saw on his way out that her door was open but she was not there.

Tony paused as they passed and looked into the empty office. 'Well, thanks again and I'll see you when you drop the transcripts off.' They continued walking to the reception. 'Best of luck and remember what I said about going back to law school. If I can help you with anything, let me know.' He shook Darren's hand with a warm, firm grip.

Darren was wondering what to do about Rachel – whether or not he might leave a message – when he heard Tony ask Carol where she was.

'She left about half an hour ago.'

'Did she say where she was going?'

'To a meeting.'

'Well, did she say when she was getting back?'

'No. My job is to answer the phones. Not to keep tabs on our legal staff.'

'You are supposed to know where everyone is.'

'She said that she was going to a meeting. See,' Carol waved her hand. 'It is here on the board. "Meeting".'

Tony stormed back to his office. He didn't like not knowing where Rachel was. He always knew where Beth Ann would be. She was always contactable, except when she was working in the prison. But even then he knew exactly where she was.

He was particularly on edge since Simone had decided to visit her grandmother. He had steadfastly refused to take her back to the old mission, even when she was little, had always insisted that his mother travel to Sydney to see them. He should have known he could not stop his daughter from going there now she was an adult. The wonder was that she had never wanted to go there sooner. In the past, her friends, studies and boyfriends kept her happy in Sydney. Now, it was out of his hands.

A deep dread had lurked within him ever since, with defiant eyes, she announced she was going. He was in no position to challenge her, to command her to stay. And he could only hope that she would be shielded from the truth that he had tried to keep from her, that he himself had tried to forget. 'I don't want you talking to her about Emily,' he had told his mother sternly.

'I'm not going to lie to her if she asks,' his mother had replied frankly.

'She won't ask if you don't bring it up, will she?'

In the end he had extracted a promise of silence from her. But still, he had been restless, short-tempered, especially with Rachel, whose unexplained absence was really ticking him off. It was all getting too complicated. Sure, he loved the passion of it, was besotted with her, but now that he had let it get so out of hand there were times when it made him miserable.

He stared at the computer screen, unable to concentrate. He'd always wanted people to admire him and he had a knack for getting others to follow his lead. He could read people and knew how to tailor his remarks and his persona to his audience. It was one of Tony Harlowe's Survival Rules: 'Play on people's need to believe'. This he had done, creating a kind of cult following – Tony Harlowe, Aboriginal activist and intellectual.

He'd done it with Rachel. She was young and looked up to him, was captivated when he spoke to her, could argue in detail with him about the more complex cases they were working on. She would listen carefully, attentively, as he went through speeches he was about to give. He had, perhaps unwittingly, but easily, slipped into a relationship with her that was beyond sexual. And the fact that he had been imagining leaving Beth Ann for her was testament to the depth of his feelings for her.

But the thought of the possible fallout of his actions made him sick. Beth Ann was so loyal, so kind-hearted, so trusting. He had known that the day he met her. Fragile and slight but her face so warm, not just beautiful but tender. He had loved her so desperately and the two times she had refused to marry him had only made him desire her more. He had known then that she was a light for him, that despite her slight frame, despite her timidity, she was solid. He could rely on her. She could help him forget the past and make the future that he had always wanted for himself. And she had done just that. Unquestioningly. Uncomplainingly.

Speaking with Darren had reminded him of everything that had been achieved since the Tent Embassy. And he had been able to be a part of that, to be a voice, a force. He mattered. His opinion was sought. His presence requested.

And Beth Ann had been there all the time. She had run his house, made sure his daughter was raised properly – his perfect, beautiful daughter. She never tried to take the credit for the things he had achieved which would have been harder, maybe impossible, if she had not been there behind the scenes, supporting him. The attraction of a partnership with an attractive, dynamic young Aboriginal lawyer who could also be an intellectual companion was a tempting fantasy. But Beth Ann had been there for him for all those decades and he owed her. Not just owed her but, despite Rachel, despite his lust, he did love her. She was – he had to admit it – still his light.

He felt the deepest wash of guilt for this situation he had gotten himself into, and for his deceitfulness. He had always tried to be honest with Beth Ann. Yes, he had been unfaithful and that brought with it a network of lies but he never had to wear the mask with her, never had to pretend with her that he was someone he wasn't. He never had to play on her need to believe. He never had to be Tony Harlowe, community leader. With Beth Ann, he revealed more of himself than to anyone else. And she had accepted him, had believed in him. Even seeing him without the mask, she had chosen to love him.

At that moment, he just wanted to be with her, at home, in the sanctuary Beth Ann kept for him. To kiss her on her forehead. To feel her body fold into his.

That was where he wanted to be. He would tell Rachel as soon as he could that it had all been a big mistake. She would always have a place in his heart but he could no longer keep deceiving his wife.

28

'Bet you were surprised that I called,' Patricia said as she opened the door to let Rachel Miles into her apartment.

'I wasn't even aware that you knew who I was,' Rachel replied. When Carol Turner had put the call through to her that afternoon, Rachel had been more than surprised, had suspected that Carol had made a mistake.

'Look, I know you must be very busy but I was hoping you might have time to come over and see me,' Patricia had said.

'Of course.'

'Tonight at five?'

And here she was, wondering why she had been summoned.

Patricia Tyndale had been a hero to Rachel since she was a teenager and started becoming interested in Aboriginal issues. She bought the Aboriginal community newspapers and Patricia was always some-where in them. Rachel had even quoted her in her essays at university and had listed her, whenever she was asked, as one of her role models – along with Tony Harlowe.

Patricia ushered her to the small table in the lounge room. 'Do you smoke?'

'No.'

'Good. It will kill you.' Patricia lit her cigarette and, after a long breath out, added, 'It's good you young people don't smoke like we did in our day. It's a filthy habit but I haven't been able to kick it. It is my only vice though.'

'One isn't bad. And I think young people have plenty of other vices that are just as awful.'

'What's yours?'

'I don't have one. I don't drink much. I don't smoke. I don't gamble. I don't take drugs. Maybe my vice is that I live a boring, sheltered life.'

Patricia looked at her contemplatively.

'Tell me about your parents.'

'They are as boring as I am. Both school teachers. I have a brother. We are both adopted. I only found out who my birth mother was when I went to uni, but she had already passed away. I have an aunt. I've seen her once. She couldn't or wouldn't tell me where I was from or who my father was.' Rachel paused. 'But she did confirm that I was Aboriginal.'

'You must think I'm a nosey old bitch.'

'No. Of course not,' Rachel said. 'I've always admired you. I was really thrilled that you wanted to see me. Surprised but thrilled.'

Patricia took another long drag on her cigarette.

'It always makes me nervous when people say they admire me. Makes me worried that they'll be disappointed.' She stubbed out her cigarette. 'And I am glad to hear that you were thrilled about my calling you when you have no idea what it was that I wanted to see you about.'

Rachel could have been taken aback but the wry smile on Patricia's face suggested that she was being lighthearted.

'Would you like something. Tea? Coffee?'

'Just water. A little late for caffeine.'

'You really don't have any vices.'

There was silence until Patricia continued. 'I know I might not have sounded gracious when you paid me that compliment about looking up to me.' She placed a glass of water in front of Rachel and resumed her chair. 'I've never been comfortable with that. I'm not good at it. But I do like to take an interest in what the young people in the community are doing and if they need my advice or support or help, I'm very happy to give it. I realised when your name was mentioned to me that I didn't know who you were and I thought I would introduce myself.'

'Well, I really appreciate that,' Rachel replied earnestly. 'It's a little hard sometimes. My parents are great. I have a wonderful relationship with them but, you know, there are some things I can't talk to them about because they wouldn't understand.'

'I suspected something like that when I first heard of you. I thought you might have been adopted. Makes it hard to find a place here.'

'I didn't have much contact with Aboriginal people when I was growing up. In fact, I had none. But working on Aboriginal issues was what I always wanted to do. And while I'm so happy doing what I'm doing now, there are times when I feel like an outsider. I didn't quite fit in when I was growing up away from the Aboriginal community but I don't fit in here either.'

Patricia lit another cigarette.

'We're a tough mob. You'd think with all that we have been through with the removal policy – whole families torn apart, sometimes three, even four generations – that we'd be a little more welcoming of our own who grew up under those kind of circumstances and want to reconnect. We're a hard club to break into.'

She paused and looked out at the window. Rachel instinctively knew to let Patricia finish her thoughts.

'Most of us have so little. Some of us have never had very much. We're suspicious of anybody who comes along as though they are going to take everything away from us. It's a mentality that's ingrained in some people. I'm not making excuses for it when I say it's understandable considering the lives many of our people have led. It's just human nature.'

Patricia turned back to Rachel. 'I want to tell you this. Aboriginal people judge you most on what you do. If you keep working for what you honestly think is the best thing for our community, they will come to respect you for that and you will gain acceptance when you have proven yourself in that way. So don't be disheartened by the fact that many will be a bit stand-offish. While we don't bring the welcome mat out easily, we don't close the door on those who have done the hard yards. We give them respect, albeit begrudgingly sometimes.'

'That means a lot to me, to hear you say that,' Rachel said earnestly, sincerely.

Rachel marvelled at Patricia's face. The high cheeks, the barely lined skin – except around the eyes – and the large, almond-shaped brown eyes. Classically beautiful.

'But look, Rachel, that isn't the only reason I invited you over.' She gave the wry smile again and looked at Rachel firmly for some time, long enough for Rachel to become nervous.

'I've heard the rumours about you and Tony.'

Rachel flushed pink.

'I don't want to say anything about that. I didn't bring you over here to judge you or dress you down. I only want to say something to you. Because you are young. And you are bright. And you are part of our community.'

Patricia paused, lighting another cigarette.

'What I want to say to you is that you do not need the approval of other people to be Aboriginal. Don't let others make you feel that you are, as they usually say, "not Aboriginal enough" or "a coconut" – you know, brown on the outside and white on the inside.'

'Yes, I have heard that,' Rachel said grimly.

'Don't let anyone tell you that because you are educated, because you are middle class, because you were adopted out or because you do not know who your father is that you are not Aboriginal. It's an insidious, unkind way of trying to bring our own people down. It's behaviour I detest.'

Rachel could feel the tingling welling of tears in her eyes. She willed herself not to cry with the humiliation of knowing that people were aware that she was having an affair. Here, with Patricia Tyndale, someone she so admired, she felt naked, ashamed.

'And I detest it because it can make young people feel insecure. Make them feel as though they need to prove themselves in ways that no Aboriginal person should have to. And they can make misguided choices. I've seen it too many times. I didn't sit in that Tent Embassy and get myself beaten up by coppers so that we could all stay uneducated and poor, dependent on government handouts.'

Rachel was lost for words.

'As I said, I'm not judging you, Rachel. I just wanted to give you this advice. You can take it or ignore it as you choose. What you do with your life is none of my business. But ours is a small community, one where some of us make matters that are none of our business, our business. And as you will find out about me, I am nothing if not a woman with a lot of opinions which I like to wrap up as advice.'

The days were getting longer, it was still warm and, while the walk home would take about an hour and a half, Rachel had a lot to think about.

Just after she started working at the Aboriginal Legal Service, Robynne, who had continued to work to help her to find her birth family, rang to say that she had good news. She had found Rachel's aunt. Thelma Ryan. She lived in the western suburbs and was willing to meet with Rachel.

She took the long drive there with Robynne. The address was for a light-green weatherboard house, no gardens but a wire fence and two kitchen chairs on the concrete verandah. Inside smelt of poverty and stale cigarette smoke.

Aunt Thelma was a rotund woman with a chubby face, sad dark eyes and large moles on her upper cheeks. She lived with Bill, a skinny, pale man who had a thick caramel beard and fading tattoos on his arms and his knuckles, and a tattooed tear drop on his outer eye.

Aunt Thelma opened the door. She took the flowers and chocolates that Rachel had brought and ushered her in. 'I'm so nervous. I need a drink.'

Thelma drank straight from the beer bottle. She offered one to Rachel and to Robynne but both declined. It was only ten in the morning.

'S'pose you want me to tell you about your mother. You look like her. In the eyes and the mouth. And that long dark hair. She was very vain about her hair. I remember once when we was in the home and the sister cut it off because she had lice. Broke her heart. She cried and cried.'

Thelma took another sip of her beer. 'She was a drinker, like me, your mother. But she only came to love the booze after she lost you. She was living out at Coonamble then.'

'Can you tell me much about where our family is from?' Rachel had asked.

'Well,' replied her aunt, looking into the distance, 'we weren't much interested in that. Only brought me grief, being an Abo. Do you think you would have been taken from your mother if you'd been white?'

'Were you all from Coonamble?'

'No. We were from out Gilgandra way. We lived by the riverbank. Dad used to follow the fruit picking and then we would come back to Gilgandra when the season was over. He was a hard man. Always giving us a good hiding. And giving Mum one, too.' Thelma took another swig.

'When she died, we went to live with our Uncle Joe at Cobar. It was the first time I lived in a house but we became too wild for him. He was old and not too well so we quickly got out of hand.'

'Do you know anything about my father?'

'Nope. Can't tell you nothin' about that. Your mother never said. She went to work in Sydney for a while and she came back to see me. Bill and I was in Peak Hill then 'cause he was driving the trucks. When she arrived she was already knocked up with you. And she never said. She always looked real sad when she was asked, and you know us, we always ask what we want to know, not shy about that.' She started laughing with a hearty croak that cracked into a deep coughing fit. When Thelma recovered herself, she took another big gulp of beer.

'She would say, "This child has no father, only God. He'll take care of her." Don't know why she believed that 'cause God sure didn't seem to be around much when we were young, especially not when we were living with our dad. And I have to say, I haven't seen a lot of God since then either. Mind you, Bill has been a blessing to me, haven't you, love?'

Bill, who hadn't said a word, just shrugged his shoulders.

'And he got this for you. Show her, love.'

Bill pushed a paper envelope across the table. Rachel opened it and saw it was a photo of a young woman with long black hair, a bright smile and a short dress.

'That's your mother. Bill got it copied down at the shop. See, he's real thoughtful.' Bill just shrugged and averted his gaze.

'Oh thank you. Thank you, Bill. Thank you, Thelma. I can't tell you what this means to me,' cried Rachel as she cradled the photograph in her hands.

When it was time for Rachel to leave, she stood to give Thelma a hug. Thelma was a little unsteady on her feet and slurred a little as she spoke, 'You come back here and visit your aunty. And bring some photos of you when you was a baby. I'd love to see that.'

'Sure. Of course. Anything I can do for you, you only need to ask.'

'Have you got a twenty for your aunty?'

Rachel looked in her purse. She had been to the bank before she had come.

'I'm sorry. I only have a fifty.'

'That'll do.' Rachel did not know how to say no.

She also did not know how to explain to Robynne why she could not stop crying the whole way home. She had not expected a happy ending. And her aunt had been welcoming even though she clearly had her own problems. But rather than feeling as though something had been discovered, the void within her seemed larger and rawer than ever before.

Before the encounter with her aunt, Rachel hadn't intended for anything to happen between her and Tony. She had thought it best that the chemistry that charged the air between them should remain unexplored.

She had wanted to belong, had wanted to feel like she had found her place, where she fitted in, and been jealous of the ease at which someone like Simone could say 'I'm Tony Harlowe's daughter' and everyone would know who she was, where she came from, who she was related to. How envious she was of people who could confirm their identity, their place in the network of kinship.

She was often asked by her clients, 'Who are your mob?' She could only vaguely answer and it always made her feel like they looked at her with a little more suspicion, as though she was not one of them. And for reasons she couldn't explain, being with Tony Harlowe made her feel closer to this world she so badly wanted to find her place in.

29

Tony felt an urgency to find Beth Ann. He walked through the hallway, to the kitchen where she was most often to be found this time of the evening. He hadn't rung to say he would be home early, and in the last months there had been few nights when that was the case. No wonder she had not started dinner. But he could hear her in the house, could tell she was there. He smiled warmly to himself as he walked towards the laundry.

She had her back to him and was standing over the ironing board folding clothes. He stood still, watching her deftly work. She had been the heart of his family, he thought. She had brought everything together. She had made him strong. She, and no one else, had helped him leave behind his past, especially the events of that awful night – and had helped him become who he was. Not a perfect man, he knew. But he was, despite all his flaws, the best man he could be because of Beth Ann's love.

'Hello, you,' he said as he moved closer to her, moving to wrap his arms around her, to hold her close.

Beth Ann shrugged Tony's arms off. 'Don't,' she said in a voice so low it barely sounded like hers.

'What's wrong, love?' he had asked her, surprised. Beth Ann had never pulled away from him.

'I'm done,' she growled in the same low tone.

Tony looked at her, confused. He had never seen her like this. There was a hardness to her face. It seemed greyish. There was no light.

'What's wrong?' he asked, his tone attempting to be soothing.

'You know what's wrong,' she replied.

And he did. He could read it. He knew it from the acid burn in his stomach and the slow heat coming to his temples. Had Simone said something, let something slip? He panicked. How much could Beth Ann know? Deny it, he told himself. Whatever she'd been told, he could argue his way out of it.

'I'm not a mind reader,' he said.

'You've been seeing someone else. You're having an affair.'

And there it was, hanging in the air between them.

'No.' He could hear the hollowness in his voice.

'Don't treat me like an idiot.' Her voice was now sharp, the flash of fire in it.

'Who told you? What did they say?' Tony demanded.

'I can't live like this anymore.'

'Wait, Beth Ann. Come on. Don't I get a chance to defend myself?' he pleaded.

'Well?' she demanded. 'Defend yourself then.'

Tony was thrown.

'There is no one else. Of course people talk. There's always gossip. You know how it is. But that doesn't mean it's true. Whatever has been said to you, tell me what it is and who said it because I can promise you there's no basis for it. There's always some false rumour or other about somebody but they're usually baseless. Of course people are jealous of me. There are lots of malicious things said. But it's gossip. It doesn't mean it's true.'

'You really do think that I'm stupid, don't you?'

'I don't. I love you most in the world. Just tell me what was said and who said it and I'll sort it out.' He'd been practising what he'd say if Simone had said something, had planned how he would explain.

'No one told me anything. I rang the hotel when you were in Lightning Ridge and when I asked for your room the operator said that "Mr and Mrs Harlowe" were not answering.'

Tony felt a blessed hint of relief. Maybe, he thought, he could win this.

'Beth Ann, there was no one else in my room. Clearly this woman on the front desk made a mistake.

How can you possibly think that I would do something like that to you? The woman who put you through to my room must have been an idiot. She obviously got it wrong. It could easily happen that she would make a mistake like that. Love, I can't believe that you would take that as proof that I was with someone else.'

Beth Ann stood glaring at him. 'Well, if all you say is true, what is your explanation for this?' Beth Ann picked up a bra – black and lacy – from where it had been thrown to the floor.

He could feel the colour drain from his face.

'It's Simone's,' he said.

'Then explain why it's not her size and why I found it in your overnight bag, the one you took to Lightning Ridge.'

Tony had no answer. The burning acid feeling was consuming his whole body. He'd been caught out. There was no explanation. On the spot, he couldn't think of a plausible one.

Something else stopped him. It was in Beth Ann's face, her eyes. There was something different about her, something resolved, hard.

'Enough, Tony. Enough,' she said quietly, handing the incriminating evidence to him. 'Go,' she said. 'Go to her now. I don't want you near me.' And then, more softly, 'I can't stand to look at you.'

Tony grabbed his overnight bag. He tossed in a few belongings – his toiletries and some clothes. Exactly what he would have taken if he was leaving for one of his regular trips away. Except he left saying nothing to Beth Ann. She was still at the back of the house. He was glad. He could not bear to see her face.

Beth Ann walked down the hallway and put the chain on the door. She unplugged the phone. She wasn't hungry but made herself eat some avocado and tomato on toast and poured a large glass of wine. She drew a long bath and put on her best nightdress.

She changed the sheets before she slipped into bed. Clean sheets would mean no Tony Harlowe in her bed. No hair, no skin left behind.

While she waited in the dark for sleep to come, she replayed the events that had unfolded that afternoon. How quickly he had surrendered. How swiftly he had acted on her command to leave.

Beth Ann was not hysterical, not even sad. She'd probably feel more fragile in the morning when she woke up alone, she thought. Then the floodgates would open and she would weep.

She planned to make an appointment tomorrow with a solicitor. She wanted the house sold and she would take half of the assets they had accumulated over their life together. She would move swiftly because she knew she should get matters finalised while Tony was in the throes of new love, while he was planning his own new life. Each step she took towards her own independence would make the one she took after it that much easier.

30

THE OLD MISSION

The heat seems to stretch time in this town. Its plumes drift up from the bubbling tarred roads. In the generous yards with modest homes, the grass is parched brown.

I've been here a week, staying in my grandmother's weatherboard house on the old mission. The rooms have the musty smell of dust resting on a lifetime of possessions and there is a constant click-click-click of the fan. Nan keeps the radio on and it twangs country music most of the day. She sits on her chair in the noon-time heat. She has shown me how to make real lemonade and we sit and sip from long, chipped glasses.

'This is nice, Nan, Spending time with you.'

'Well, I would come and see you more but it is harder the older I get. I need to be near my things. And I don't like the bus. I feel like a sardine in a tin – with a whole load of white sardines.'

I laugh. I wonder why I have never been here before. 'Why does Dad never come home?'

She eyes me warily. 'That's something you will have to ask him about. Always filled with the questions, aren't you?'

Suddenly the front door opens and a small whirlwind in the form of my cousin Melanie enters the room. Her younger sister Amanda slips in quietly behind her. They are not technically my cousins. My grandmother and their grandfather were brother and sister but this is a tight-knit community. I'd never met them until I came out to visit this time. My mother would send them the clothes I grew out of as a child and Nan sent some pictures once of the girls prancing around in the ill-fitting garments. 'Did you bring us any stuff?' had been Melanie's greeting when we first met.

'I've had a gutful of this fucking heat.' Melanie flops herself down in a chair. 'I can't believe I have to work tonight but at least there is air-conditioning there.'

Amanda has a baby with her and she has unfolded a blanket on the ground at Nan's feet and rests the baby on it. The baby is Melanie's but Amanda quietly, uncomplainingly, seems to do all the work.

'Where do you work?' I ask politely.

'In the nursing home on the other side of town.'

I suppress a laugh. I could imagine Melanie telling a resident who wanted something to 'go get it your fucking self'. But the baby is her fourth child and I admire her determination to provide for them. Like many people with brash exteriors, she has a good heart.

'How's that father of yours?' Nan asks the girls.

'He was in a right mood this morning,' Melanie chuckles. 'He says that if the Housing Department don't fix the plumbing this week he is going to burn the whole place down.'

A smile creeps across Nan's face. 'It's those bureaucrats from Sydney. They come out here on the plane, all clean clothes and shiny hair and a year later they leave on a plane, looking shabbier and a whole lot less shiny. Problems here ain't so easy to fix with lots of fine talk. We need to pay doctors and teachers more or they ain't gonna come out here for the long haul. And we need some money to fix that school hall.'

Melanie and Amanda nod in agreement so Nan continues. 'And by the time they get to know who is who, who to talk to and who to ignore, they are packing their gear and heading back to the city. Just when we have finally got them trained. This last one that came out from the Aboriginal Affairs Department reminded me of the mission manager we had here when I was a girl. We used to call him gawu.'

The two girls started to giggle.

'Gawu?' I ask.

'Yeah. It's the word for egg in the old language,' Nan explains.

I still don't understand and, reading my face, she continues. 'He would sit around all day and do nothing and everyone would run around making sure he was looked after very nicely. Like an egg.'

'That, and he was an undeveloped life form.' Melanie laughs heartily at her own joke and I can't help but join in.

The baby starts to cry. Amanda lifts him up to Nan and she settles him down in her fleshy arms. I look at how gently she cradles him, how instinctively she knows how to keep him quiet. I wonder yet again why Dad never comes home.

Nan is gazing at the baby she has just lulled to sleep when she says, 'Why don't you two take your cousin out to the cemetery later today. It's too hot for me in this heat but the graves need to be tidied. I've some flowers for your mother and for Emily.'

A photograph of Emily, a studio portrait, sits on the wall opposite Nan. Dark eyes and pouty mouth – made beautiful with the same features that made Dad handsome. Beside Emily's portrait sits one of my grandfather, George. Handsome as well, dressed in a suit. The photograph had been coloured by hand but has faded.

Nan's eyes flick to Emily's picture as she speaks and I realise how strange it is to hear the name my father never mentions – 'Emily' – said aloud. Mum once explained how he hated to talk about her death and it was a family agreement among the three of us never to speak of it. Now I suddenly wanted to go to see her grave, this mysterious woman who Nan loved. And Dad must have loved her too otherwise her death would not have pained him so.

'It's too bloody hot to go dancing around the dead,' Melanie swaggers.

'Go later in the day. And have some respect for the old people,' Nan rebukes her sharply.

'All right. But we're taking her car.' Melanie points at me.

When we pull up at the cemetery, the heat has relented. It's still warm but not too oppressive to move.

You can learn a lot about a town by the cemetery. We walk past the graves of the babies. 'Died seven months. With the angels now.' 'Died three days old. Always in our hearts.' And one grave: 'Died five years old. Our light. Our boy.' The grave is covered with tiny tin and plastic cars, with whistles and other small toys. The odd, colourful display – like a Christmas tableau – is a tribute to inconsolable grief.

We walk further past lines of granite and marble headstones. Some have one side filled with the other side patiently waiting for the spouse to join them. Here lies Pop. Husband of Wilma.

Melanie talks as we go, noticing my interest. 'That one there is for Wilma Patterson's husband. I bet she talked him into that bloody grave. She runs the canteen up at the school. She's an ox. Old man will be waiting a long time for her to join him.'

Wilma ordered the headstone so clearly she knows that is where she wants to be when she goes. The cynical side of me wonders whether her husband wanted the same thing. Still, how comforting it must be to know where you are heading, to know there is a place for you, to know that there is someone who will rest beside you for eternity.

Melanie gives me an oral history of the other graves. There are several young men and women who've been killed in car accidents – friends from school, even two cousins. 'It's the mix of the grog and the long distances between towns,' she says. And the recklessness of youth, that feeling of invincibility that teenagers possess, I think to myself.

We arrive at the grave of Melanie's mother. Melissa 'Bloss' Trindall. Died 57. Beloved wife of John, mother of Melanie, Jack, Jason, Philip, Sarah and Amanda.

'Dad called her Blossom and it got shortened to Bloss. I sure miss her. There's plenty of stuff I wanted to ask her before the cancer finally took her off. But at least I can go to Nan for most of it.' She stares at the grave and a softness comes into her face. She pauses a while in her own thoughts.

'There,' she says finally, pointing three graves down. 'The one with the white angel on it is Emily's.'

I walk over and place the flowers Nan gave me from her garden, now wilted in the heat. Beloved daughter of George and Frances. Beloved sister of Tony. Died 1972. Aged 17.

'So young to be taken by an accident,' I say, thinking of the inexplicable cruelty of losing someone you love in circumstances you cannot control. It must be one of the most disempowering, soul-crushing things in the world. No wonder Dad's had such problems coming to terms with it. No wonder the sadness never leaves Gran's eyes.

Melanie has turned towards me, her hands on her hips.

'She wasn't killed in an accident,' she corrects, as though I am soft-headed. 'She killed herself.'

31

If Beth Ann had any doubts about acting quickly to settle things with Tony they were silenced when the news trickled back to her that Tony was indeed living with another woman.

Not everyone who had brought her information had intended to be kind.

'Beth Ann,' Liz Briggs had said, 'I am so sorry to hear how Tony had treated you. After all these years you had stood by him and now to be left for someone who is younger than your daughter. It must be so humiliating.'

The barely disguised joy of some about the break-up of her marriage had surprised her, but so had the generosity of others. Just two days after the split – how quickly the black grapevine works when it has some gossip – she received a call offering her a job teaching the literacy bridging course at the Aboriginal college.

'You are just being kind,' Beth Ann had said.

'This is not sympathy. We need you. Our last teacher quit last week. Patricia Tyndale, who's on our board, recommended you. Honestly, you'd be doing us a huge favour.'

And so she had accepted. Not long after, the university down the road offered her some tutoring on their bridging course. Starting next year in February.

She'd been touched that, though she was white, people had looked after her. She had never pushed to be accepted and now, when help was most appreciated, these acts of thoughtfulness made her feel like she had been included.

One week without Tony and she had two part-time jobs and set the wheels in motion for a property settlement. She calculated she could buy a small flat, invest the rest and work part-time. She had never been extravagant, was the kind of woman who did not dye her hair and liked bright, classic clothes, not necessarily expensive ones. She also decided that she would move to the other side of the harbour. She didn't want to keep running into people in the street and find herself the object of their pity.

She'd never expected marriage to be all romance. She had been realistic about it all along, had expected to have to compromise and to concede. Marriage, she had thought, took two people with a firm resolve to make it work. Both she and Tony had lost that resolve now.

Even with Christmas looming she felt scarce regret that she would be spending it on her own – perhaps with Simone but not with Tony. She had already given herself the best present: her freedom.

It only remained to tell Simone. 'Best if you do it,' Tony had said when they spoke on the phone yesterday morning. 'She'll take it better coming from you.'

It was commonly understood that a divorce is hard on the children. Even adult children. Beth Ann wondered how much harder the news would be for Simone when she found out that her father was living with someone only slightly younger than she was.

Or would she be surprised? Since Tony had left and Beth Ann had been reminded of how swiftly gossip flew around the neighbourhood, she began to suspect that the rift she had seen between father and daughter could be explained by this new relationship. For Tony to have moved in, it must have been going on for some time and have been serious. If Tony couldn't hide it from his wife, he probably hadn't hid it from many people.

Carl Jung once said, 'Nothing has a stronger influence psychologically on their environment, and especially on their children, than the unlived lives of their parents.' Beth Ann had remembered it because she thought it explained a lot about her own childhood – the impact of watching her mother's happiness smothered by an unhappy marriage. Surely she owed Simone the example of being a woman who makes certain that her life is fully lived.

32

'You knew that Melanie would tell me the truth about Emily.'

I have just finished putting the last of the washed dishes away. Nan is sitting in her chair, looking at the pictures of Emily and George on the wall in front of her.

It is two days since I visited the cemetery and I can think of nothing else. Finding a family secret raises more questions than it answers. I have plenty and have been biding my time waiting for the right moment to ask Nan some of them.

'Is that why Dad never wanted to come back here?'

'It was my fault that he carried it so hard. I raised him to be strong. When George died Tony was so young but I always made him believe he was the man of the house, that he had responsibility for us all. He did look after us too. But when that terrible thing happened, he blamed himself for not protecting Emily. For not being able to protect us.'

I sit quietly next to her, waiting patiently for her to reveal more.

'George and I knew that life was tough if you were black and we kind of accepted it because we grew up with racism all the time. When we finally came to this mission was the first time I had shoes. I remember how proud I was of 'em and they were really just cardboard. But see, back then, blacks were given so little, we were so grateful for any mean thing we got. And yet we all worked so hard all the time. I wanted life to be different for Tony and Emily.

'Tony would never accept that he wasn't as good as anyone else. I'm proud of him for that. Always held his head high. Thought he was as good as any white person and no one was going to deny him anything. So when it happened, it shook his pride and crushed him.'

She pauses for a while. Again lost in a memory. I think of my father and for the first time here with Nan, in this place where he grew up, I appreciate how much he has made of his life. He was forever pushing me to take opportunities and I am chastened to realise that I have rarely thought about the barriers – greater than any that faced me – that he overcame.

'So I understood why he had to leave,' Gran says, breaking me from my thoughts. 'I understood why he never wanted to talk about it. I understood why he never wanted to come home. And I also understand why it is so important for him to do things to help our people. I understand why he drives himself so hard. I understand why he feels better when people admire him, why he needs to be loved.'

Nan is quiet again but I know she has not finished speaking. I am glad Patricia taught me about the silences when people talk and I respect them now.

'And he did do good, you know. All his generation, those angry young men and women who said enough and demanded their rights, our rights. They made a difference. These houses weren't built out here until after they started talking about rights. And many of us were too shy to ask for them. Didn't know how. Some said they should be quiet, not rock the boat. But we are so much better off now than we were back then before they were marching in the streets. Even if we still have a long way to go. But,' she turns to look at me directly and raises her finger, shaking it slightly, 'if he thinks it was hard on him, that thing that happened, what they did, imagine how hard it was on those of us who stayed. And how hard it was on Emily. In the end, it was too hard on her. She just couldn't take it after what they did to her.'

'Who were they and what did they do to her?'

'Those boys raped her down by the river. They might as well have killed her right then and there.'

I feel a chill down my spine. Raped? Nan's face has hardened. I sense that she will say nothing more.

There is a trickle of sweat on her brow, glistening in the sun.

'Would you like a glass of lemonade?' I ask gently.

She nods, still looking at the photographs of Emily and George.

When I return with the cool glass, I ask one last question.

'Nan, what was Emily like?'

Nan smiles. 'She was like a little bird, a little sparrow. Quiet but busy. Always wanted to help. She adored her brother. Would have done anything for him. She was the kind that would have done anything for anyone. She was like an angel on this earth.'

Nan takes a long drink. 'There was something about your mother, her goodness, and the sense that she was fragile, that always reminded me of my little Emily.'

The telephone rings. I am more mobile than Nan so I have taken to answering it.

It's my mother. 'We were just talking about you. Were your ears burning?'

'No. What were you talking about? Have you spoken to your father?'

'No, I haven't spoken to Dad. And we were saying nice things about you.' Her questions make me suspicious. 'What's wrong, Mum?'

'Nothing. Nothing. Everything is fine. Just fine. I wanted to ring before you come back and let you know that your father and I have decided to separate.'

The chill I felt upon hearing about Emily's rape is back.

'Why? What has he done?'

'It's a mutual decision. I'm staying in the house for the time being and he has moved out.'

'Already? When?'

'Just over a week ago. The night after you left to visit your Nan.'

'Over a week ago. And no one told me?'

'I didn't want you to worry about us.'

'I'll come home,' I say.

'No, no. I'm fine. You stay with your Nan. She rarely sees you and it must mean a lot to her to have you visiting. There is no need to come home early.'

'Where's Dad gone?'

'He's staying with – a friend.'

I don't ask any more. I suspect it is Rachel and if Mum knows she clearly doesn't want to tell me. If she doesn't know, I'm not about to tell her.

'Should I let Nan know? Or should I keep it a secret until you are sure that this is what you really want.'

'You can let her know now, if you find the right time.'

'That was Mum on the phone,' I say, returning to my seat next to Nan. 'She and Dad have split up.'

'I know. I heard.'

'I was in the other room. I thought you were hard of hearing.'

Nan ignores my attempt at humour. She looks past me.

'I love your mother like she was my own daughter.'

'She's very fond of you too.'

'But that son of mine . . . I know. I hear. I don't like it.' Nan finishes the last of her lemonade. 'I always worried that one day he would do something to lose her.'

'Seems like that day has finally come,' I say glumly.

'Well, it took longer to get here than I thought it would.'

We sit in silence for some time. The room starts to darken but neither of us stir. Even though I had caught my father out, it never occurred to me that my parents would separate. I have never imagined them apart.

Finally, Nan tells me to put the television on so we can watch the news. We stare at the screen but my mind is full of my mother, my father and Emily.

33

I wake up early the next morning. I can tell from the light that it is just after dawn. I have had a fitful sleep with so much on my mind. Why was what happened to Emily kept such a secret? Why was there shame around her being raped? Why was there silence about her suicide? Is that why my father decided not to come back here? Why did he feel the need to protect me from what had happened? Why did he think I was not capable of understanding the truth?

Now, awakening, I am even more agitated. How could he cheat on my mother? She had been the best of wives to him. How could he be so selfish, so indulgent to have an affair? How could he throw away everything Mum has given him?

I am furious and can no longer lie in bed. I tiptoe to the phone in Nan's living room and dial Dad's mobile. It rings several times and I am about to give up when he answers.

'How could you do what you've done to Mum?' I demand.

'Simone?'

'Yes, it's me. And I want to know how you could treat Mum the way you have?'

'I'm not happy about this situation either.' His voice has the thick sound of being woken from a deep sleep. 'Your mother wanted me out of the house.'

I am taken aback a little. Mum had said it was a mutual decision and I had assumed Dad had left her. But I think of the embrace I caught him in with Rachel. I think of the times he would bring his friend Liz along to the movies with us. My anger boils again.

'Well, you must have deserved it.'

He is silent and I wonder whether he is still on the line. Finally he speaks, 'I am not at all happy about things between me and your mother and I understand why you're upset about them.'

What could he know, I think to myself. Could he know how betrayed I felt when he used me to cover for his infidelity? Could he know what it must be like for Mum who was always there for him but now is discarded for someone younger than her daughter? How could he know these things?

'I don't understand you,' I say. I mean it as an accusation of his failure to understand how his actions have affected me and have injured Mum.

'Well,' he pauses. There is tiredness in his voice. 'I don't understand myself either sometimes.'

Dad's openness about his misery startles me. I expected him to be defensive, to hide, to blame someone else. In his candour, I can see that he is unhappy and that he knows that he is the cause of it. Seeing him so bereft is unexpected and I find, not forgiveness, but sympathy emerging for him in my heart. My anger towards him lessens. But I still have questions.

'Dad, I need to ask you something. Not about you and Mum. About something else.'

There is silence. I can feel him bracing himself and I know that he will not be expecting me to move from interrogating him about Mum to asking questions about Emily. But I sense that now, with his guard down, with his frankness about his flaws, it might be the best time to ask him about the secrets he has tried so hard to hide. I need to understand why her death was so hard for him to face and why he had to hide the truth from me.

'I have found out that Aunt Emily killed herself. And I just want to know why you never told me.'

He takes a moment to answer. I sense his discomfort but I give him no ground and wait until he finally speaks. 'It was a very unhappy incident in my life. When someone you love takes their own life you are left with a lifetime of wondering what you could have done to have stopped it. There may have been a part of me that wanted to protect you from such unpleasant events but it has always been a very hard thing for me to deal with. That's why I never talk about it.'

My father sounds defeated. I'm unsure of what to say next. It is the first time he has revealed so much of himself to me. Until Professor Young's death I had known no one who had committed suicide. It must be one thing to deal with a death that is accidental but different to deal with one that is intentional. Did that explain the anger I had seen in Professor Young's daughter at the memorial service? Did it go some way to explaining why his family did not want his book of poetry? Death must always bring with it grief, sadness and regrets. Wondering what could have been done to prevent the death of someone you love must be a terrible burden. Death draws a curtain down on everything. There is no time to say what is unsaid.

I remember the scrapbook that Patricia had shown me with the newspaper clipping of the interview where, when asked how he would spend his last night on earth, my father said it would be with me. My anger ebbs away completely.

'Dad?'

'Yes?' He sounds wary, as if readying for another assault from me.

'Are you okay?'

He sounds surprised. 'I've been better. But I'm doing all right under the circumstances.'

Nan has stirred. She walks past me towards the kitchen.

I look at Emily's photograph. Even in the dimness of early light I can see how much she looks like my father. And at this moment, I no longer feel like judging him.

'I love you, Dad.'

'I love you, too.' He sounds confused. Perhaps relieved. But I know he means it.

I hang up and walk to the kitchen.

'I made a cup of tea,' Nan says. She's sitting at the kitchen table, a cup in front of her. An empty cup sits beside the pot for me. 'I know he's not perfect but I love him. Even with his faults he is a good man. And I'm not just saying that because I'm his mother.'

'I know, Nan,' I say meekly. I sit down next to her. 'And I'm not just saying that because I'm his daughter.'

'I understand why you're mad at him. I want to give him a kick in the pants most of the time myself.' She smiles and I grin back at her. 'But,' she becomes more serious and points a finger at me, 'despite that, he does deserve your respect. We can't abandon him just because he's not perfect.'

'I think I am starting to understand that too, Nan.'

A week and a half later, when I leave Nan's for the long drive home, I pass through the town but instead of staying on the highway I find my way down to the river, near the weir. I park in the meadow and follow the well-worn path down to the riverbank.

I look around and I wonder where it happened. There is no one around but there is plenty of movement. The wind plays with the leaves in the tall gum trees. The birds chatter and fuss. The cicadas and crickets sing in the stifling heat.

I sit down on the long grass. I listen and wait. I don't know what I am hoping to find. You need time to feel a place, to know what it's telling you. I'm at a disadvantage because the land speaks differently in the day to how it speaks in the night. It has a different spirit. In the light, it bustles with intention. It moves at night too, but it is more thoughtful. Places that seem peaceful in the day, you can almost hear them weeping in the dark.

But I do sense something unsettling. Much would have happened here. Although I am the only one here at this moment, I know all sorts of things go on at places like this along the river – children playing, fathers and sons fishing, girls sunbaking, flirting with boys, people falling in love, having first kisses. But then, in the dark, there are the evil spirits, the mi-mi men, Nan would call them. And somewhere here there are parts of Emily, a part of my father, my grandmother, perhaps even myself, left here because of the events of that one night.

Patricia Tyndale had been right. I felt renewed after my three weeks with Nan. Even with my parents' separation, I feel a serenity I have not felt before. As I leave the town, the loose gravel of the roads crunching under my tyres, I am grateful that there's a nine-hour drive back to the city. Time to collect my thoughts. To think. To enjoy the silences.

34

Over the past few weeks, Rachel has turned her meeting with Patricia Tyndale over and over in her mind, especially after Tony had turned up with an overnight bag, announcing that he had left Beth Ann. 'She knows about us,' he had said.

'Did Simone tell her?' was Rachel's first reaction.

'No. Seems she kept it to herself. I told her. I told her about us.'

His arrival on her doorstep and clear intention to move in made her anxious. They'd gone through the façade of Christmas. The ludicrousness of their situation became most apparent when she took Tony home for lunch at her parents' place. After all, she couldn't leave him brooding in the apartment. Simone had chosen to spend the day with her mother and had only committed to 'perhaps' drop by for dinner.

Her parents were pleasant with Tony, asked polite questions, made him feel welcome. But she could see that look – of worry, concern, disappointment – when they arrived. He so much older; she so young. Her mother's hug when she left was just slightly longer than usual, her father less at ease.

But even before then, when Tony had taken her out publicly, everyone had stared. She was convinced there was whispering behind their backs. She didn't like the attention and wanted to shrink from it. Tony must have sensed it too. He went out less and less. 'Let's skip this one,' he would say as an engagement loomed.

And now, as the new year approached, she felt the time had come to act. She had always had a kind of superstition that the tone of New Year's Eve sets the path for the rest of the year. There was no point in putting it off.

She'd had a dream the night before that she was lying in her bed and she had rolled off and Tony had rolled on top of her and was crushing her. She woke up with a start, catching her breath.

She'd rehearsed what she wanted to say. How Tony would respond was unknown and anticipating his reaction made her stomach tighten with anxiety. Always best to do it in the morning, she'd read somewhere. Then there is the rest of the day for other arrangements to be made. She'd already prepared.

She looked at him across the table strewn with the remains of breakfast. He was handsome, the grey streaks of hair and the lines made him more so, she had always thought. Yes, she loved him. But not enough. Not for right now. Not enough to choose this as her life. She counted to ten and took a deep breath.

'Tony, we need to talk,' she said.

'What about?' he answered warily, looking up from his paper.

'Tony, I didn't want you to leave your wife for me. It wasn't the deal we had from the start.'

'But things have changed from where we started. It's different now.'

'Look Tony, I made a mistake in getting involved with you. Not a mistake, that's not right. You are an amazing man and I love you. I'll always love you. But this relationship with you is not the best thing for me right now. And I don't think it is what is best for you either,' she added more quietly.

Tony looked stunned, as though she had sliced a knife through him. Then a cloud came over his face. His eyes became smaller, squinting. His jaw set hard.

'How dare you,' he thundered. 'How dare you do this to me. Don't you know who I am? I'll finish you. You'll never get a job in this town again. You'll be fucking nothing. Fucking nothing.'

The slam of Tony's fist on the bench top was forceful. The plates, cutlery and jam jars all rattled in its wake.

An unexpected calm came over Rachel. 'It's already over,' she said softly.

'I'll finish you at work. I'll finish you around this town.'

'That's what I meant, Tony. I'm already finished. I know that. I knew that the day your daughter saw us in your office. The way she looked at me. She knew – about you and me. And she will only ever see me as being where I am because I slept with you. Your colleagues will never take me seriously either. They're not interested in anything I say, what I have to offer, because they know I've slept with you. I topped seven classes at uni. I almost got the University Medal. But those guys you work with – and your daughter – will never be able to see past the fact that I had an affair with you.'

'I didn't mean what I said. I don't mean it.' Tony quietened, his initial panic replaced with resignation. 'I need you.'

A smile slipped onto her face. 'Tony, I would make you miserable.' She knew that breaking up with him would also mean having to find a new job. It highlighted the enormity of her mistake.

Patricia Tyndale had given her a great gift: the strength to know that she could make her own path without anyone else's approval or endorsement, on her own terms, her way. *Aboriginal people judge you on what you do . . . you will gain acceptance when you prove yourself. You do not need the approval of others to be Aboriginal.*

If she didn't start again now, it would be too late.

35

'So I'm an orphan,' I say.

'Your parents aren't dead, drama queen,' Patricia says.

'Their marriage is,' I retort and watch Patricia's lips purse.

Tanya and I are sitting at Patricia's table. The balcony door's open and we can hear the street noise from below. A gritty, light breeze drifts through.

'Were you surprised?' Tanya asks.

'Actually, I was. I just never thought Mum would kick him out. Dad's made it look as though he left but she told him to get out when she found out about the affair. She kind of surprised me. And I like this new Mum. She's really determined.'

'More power to her,' Tanya says. 'That will show him and his little squeeze.'

Unexpectedly, Patricia rises. 'Do you think Rachel

Miles would have been so vulnerable to being seduced by a man old enough to be her father if girls like you had been friendly and supportive rather than turning your spoilt noses up at her?'

She glares at us and, without looking at the cigarette packet, stretches out her arm and swoops it up, stalking out to the balcony. She closes the sliding door behind her.

Tanya and I look at each other.

'Ouch,' Tanya says, trying to make the mood lighter, but neither of us feel like laughing.

'You can always tell when she has the shits because she smokes outside. Any other time she is happy to puff away here,' I say.

'It is a strange concept that we should feel sympathy for the woman who broke your mum and dad up,' Tanya observes.

'Well, since Dad moved in with the little squ . . .' I stop myself. 'Since Dad moved in with Rachel, I have to confess, I do feel a bit sorry for her.'

'Really?'

'I can't explain it but I do.'

Tanya smiles. 'It sure took your mind off other things.'

'I haven't mentioned what's-his-name in a very long time and I don't intend to start now.'

'I know. And I'm proud of you.'

'I'm proud of you too, getting over that other what's-his-name.'

'Better off without him.'

'So you say now. But I'm glad to hear it. There are more important things to worry about.'

'Like what?' she grins.

But I want to be serious. 'You know that book Professor Young sent me before he died?'

She nods.

'And how he sent a note with it?' I pull the folded paper out of my wallet and read aloud. '. . . a love-less world is a dead world, and always there comes an hour when one is weary of prisons, of one's work, and of devotion to duty, and all one craves for is a loved face, the warmth and wonder of a loving heart.' I fold the paper up. 'It's from a book called *The Plague*, a novel about facing an untimely death and not knowing how to deal with it. I've been really puzzled about why he wrote that phrase and what it means.'

'And?'

'And I finally think I understand. It's not about craving to have "the warmth and wonder of a loving heart" that *loves you* but to *have* "the warmth and wonder of a loving heart" to be able to love others. That's what it means. That must be the message Professor Young was giving me. Maybe he lost his ability to love others. I don't know. Maybe that's the reason why his daughter was so angry with him when he died. But I know *I* don't want to lose it.'

'How could you? You have a really big heart. You're always in love.'

'I have a heart that has been quick to fall in love with ideals, with fantasies, but I've never been as willing to love realities.'

'Wow. You learnt all that at your Nan's place?'

'Yeah.' I smile back at her. 'I had a lot of time to think. And you know what else I found out?'

'What?'

'My Nan is not as deaf as she likes to pretend she is.'

The balcony door slides open and Patricia joins us again at the table. 'Well, have you two been reflecting on the errors of your ways?'

'You could say that. And we were just about to discuss when I'll go back to my studies. It's time for me to return to Boston.'

'You know that we're proud of you for what you are doing. We never had those chances. But,' she gives me a piercing look and taps a finger on the table, 'it's what you do when you get back that will be important. That's what we're waiting to see.'

Tanya and I eye each other. She winks. We are used to Patricia's lectures about our shortcomings and brace ourselves for another one.

'I'm not one of those people who thinks that you can learn more from real life than you can learn from books. I'm one of those people who believes you can learn from both. So I am not concerned that you have your head in a book all the time, Simone, but it does concern me when you are not reflective enough about what you are learning from real life.'

Tanya gives me a look that attempts, with sarcastic seriousness, to agree with her.

Patricia catches it, looks at Tanya, looks at me and then back at Tanya.

'You two are little shits,' she snaps.

Suddenly, I start laughing. Tanya starts too. Unexpectedly, Patricia joins in with her thick, throaty laugh.

36

'When was it that you women decided to be so independent?' Tony asked.

'About the same time you decided you didn't want to be denied things just because you were black,' Patricia replied, reaching for the bottle of wine.

'Why do I come here thinking you'll give me some sympathy?'

'I always know you are desperate when you turn up on my doorstep. You only come to me when you're really in trouble and because you know I'll tell you the truth. Everyone else feeds you bullshit.'

Patricia topped Tony's glass up.

'Your daughter was here yesterday with her friend Tanya.'

Tony looked glum.

'She judges me, you know.'

'I gave her a lecture about that.'

'Well, it didn't seem to do much good.'

'She's going back to her studies.'

Tony seemed to cheer. 'That's something.'

'I've never known someone to adore their father the way she adores you.'

'Not lately.'

'She's hurt but she's come a long way. What you put her through is not an easy thing for a daughter to come to terms with.'

'I know. But it hasn't been easy for me to come to terms with either.'

'That's just like you, to turn yourself into the victim.' Patricia smiled and then took a sip from her glass and eyed him. 'You're a show pony, Tony Harlowe. Always were. But you're decent too. Underneath that ego is a good man. And you can't hide that.'

'That's about the nicest thing you have ever said to me.'

'Well, don't get too comfortable. I'm not one of those people who get silly over your charms.'

Tony turned on his wicked grin. 'There was one night when you succumbed to them.'

'Don't go overstating one small kiss when we were children. And besides I was probably drunk.' Patricia stood grabbing the empty wine bottle on the table. 'Looks like we'll need another one of these if you are going to start getting sentimental.'

She avoided Tony's gaze as she busied herself in the

kitchen. She cut up some cheese and bread and foraged in her cupboards for more food.

'It's all I have for a surprise visitor,' she said as she placed the plates on the table.

Tony's mood was pleasant but quiet. He was looking down at his hands. He seemed smaller, older.

'What happened to the girl?' Patricia asked as she sat back down.

'She kicked me out. Then she packed up her office and left the Legal Service.' Tony looked down at his wine. 'I can't believe she kicked me out before New Year's Eve.'

'Yeah, no better way to start the New Year than with a kiss from someone who is secretly hoping to see the back of you.' She gave Tony her best signature wry smile.

'I hate it when you're right.'

'You must be unhappy most of the time then.'

It was his turn to smile.

'Well, Tony. It will be a new year in two days. You could make some resolutions.'

'I think we both know what they will be.'

They shared the smile of old conspirators.

'We go back, don't we?' Tony said affectionately.

'I suppose we do. You were cruel back then.'

'To you? Never. I adored you. Still do.'

Patricia ignored his banter.

'To Beth Ann. And to Arthur.'

'I loved her. I still do.'

'So did he.'

'I won.'

'I guess you did, Tony. I guess you did.'

'Are you going to judge me now?' The flare of his temper was starting to rise.

'No. It would be too much like judging myself.'

'Yes,' he said, his anger dissipating and a look of bleary affection returning. 'Mind if I stay the night?'

'So long as you don't mind sleeping on the couch.'

Tony gave a playful smile. 'Haven't forgotten after all these years, have you?'

'Seems like I have so you can't have been that good.'

Tony laughed. 'You're a cruel woman, Patricia. But I love you.'

That, thought Patricia as she sipped her wine, just about cut her heart in half. Tony had made it a habit. Hers. Beth Ann's. Arthur's. All their hearts had been cut in two by Tony Harlowe.

37

Arthur Randall had known Tony Harlowe for as long as he could remember. They were hardly close now and few people would guess how entwined their histories were. But when they were young, they had been inseparable. Running down to the river; sleeping under the night sky; hiding in the big tree from where they could see all of the mission without being seen themselves. They played football together on the same team, Tony in the centre, Arthur, smaller framed but fast, on the wing. They would practise, running up and down the fields, passing the ball to each other.

And in their shadow had been Emily. Naturally they thought she was a pest at first and would try to elude her so she would not follow them on their adventures, or allow her along only if she agreed to be their slave and do as they said. Always she was obedient, adoring them both. Their shadow.

He'd always liked Tony's bravado. There was a clear division between the blacks and the whites and while Arthur had barely understood it as a child, he had noticed it more the older he grew. Black kids and white kids rarely mixed. He liked the way that Tony was always saying things like, 'We're as good as they are, you know. Don't matter about the colour of our skin. Just look at the way we play football better than anyone else in the school. We wouldn't have won the premiership last three years running if they hadn't had us, if it was all just the whities.'

Tony always had examples of how the blacks were as good as the whites. He knew that the first cricket team to tour England was Aboriginal. That an Aboriginal cricketer, Eddie Gilbert, was the only bowler to knock the bat out of Sir Donald Bradman's hands and the only one to have bowled him for a duck. Gilbert played twenty-three matches for Queensland in the 1930s. During that time he took eighty-seven wickets at an average of twenty-nine.

He knew all the Aboriginal players in the football, could relate all the feats of Larry Cowara and Arthur Beetson. And he told Arthur how Lionel Rose became the world bantamweight champion in 1968.

'So, you tell me, how could we be inferior? Way I see it, white people secretly worry that we're better so they go out of their way to tell us that we're not.' To Arthur, Tony seemed to know about the idea of Black Power without ever having heard of it.

As Tony got older, he became even more brash, less reverent about the existing hierarchy in the town where white people had more privileges than blacks, where segregation was a way of life from the hospital to the school yard, the picture theatre, and even the cemetery. 'You enter the world segregated and you leave it the same way,' Tony would say.

The old mission was five miles out of town. It had formerly been run by the church many decades ago and had then become what was known as a reserve, land set aside for Aboriginal people where they were kept under the control of an administrator – a mission manager – and controlled by the government. While the days of the mission manager had disappeared about the time Tony and Arthur were born, all of the older people had memories of when their rations, movements, ability to work were controlled.

At night, when the old men and old women sat on their porches, talking in the evening air about the old times, Arthur and Tony liked to sit and listen. Arthur loved hearing about the old ways and was always keen to hear the stories. He liked to learn the language and hear tricks on how to catch fish or listen for birds, how to find water, which berries and flowers could be eaten, the best way to skin kangaroos and how to make string from their intestines. He liked the stories about the way the snake made the rivers because, when you went down near the river and looked at the way it wound through the landscape, it did look just like a snake had slithered through there.

He and Tony liked the stories about how people would outsmart the mission manager. His favourite was about the night Tommy Boney had wanted to go to a dance in town. He had stolen the manager's suit off the line where it was airing and put it back when he came back early in the morning, complete with a cigarette burn in the pocket.

As they grew older, he and Tony felt the tensions in the town more acutely. The police had always come to the mission whenever anything happened in town and they started recognising Tony, and to a lesser extent Arthur himself, once they reached puberty. By the time Tony was fifteen, they were regularly being stopped by the police and questioned whenever they came into town.

Tony gave as good as he got. With his smart mouth and cheeky grin he would stand tall. 'Evening Officers,' he'd say.

'You'll eat that grin, you little black bastard,' they would mutter back. Although the coppers seemed to change every year, the new ones seemed to have been told to watch out for Tony Harlowe.

By this time, Emily followed them around less. She was always helping her mother, cooking and clean-ing, working on her studies or sewing. She liked to make and mend clothes and embroider handkerchiefs. She would stitch dainty little flowers and letters, even tiny bluebirds. She stitched one for Arthur for his sixteenth birthday. It had his name in blue letters and was trimmed with white.

On her fifteenth birthday, with money he had saved that summer fruit picking, Arthur bought Emily a gold cross on a thin gold chain.

Then that night, that terrible nightmare night, changed everything. They'd heard about the way car loads of boys would take girls down to the riverbank, each taking their turn with them. But that night, when they heard the whispers in town about a gang-bang, they had not paid much attention. Neither he nor Tony thought that kind of behaviour proper but neither did they do anything to intervene.

Jenny Dixon, one of Emily's closest friends, had found them. She was frantic. 'I think they have taken Emily to the riverbank,' she panted. 'We were walking on the road out, coming into town, and the car pulled up and they dragged her in. They tried to get me too, but I was faster. When they had gone, I ran here to find you.'

Tony and Arthur didn't have to hear any more. They ran as fast as they could down to the riverbank, to the weir, where it was town folklore that the gang-bangs took place. Arthur could not remember much of the run, only the panic to find her, the dark horror creeping over them as they sped towards where they hoped Emily would be.

They saw the cars. They could hear the voices. Neither could remember much of what happened next, it was all instinct and adrenalin, but two boys took on eight and with their rage got the better of them. Tony had always been a fighter but Arthur could never explain where he got his strength from that night. It was the first and last time he ever raised his fists in anger. In the end, the whites made their way back to their cars and sped off. Tony bundled up the broken, naked body of his little sister and the two boys carried her all the way home. All Arthur could remember was the sound of Emily's sobbing. He would hear it in his worst dreams for years to come.

They rushed into Tony's house, yelled for his mother. She gasped at the bundle, and only then in the better light could they see the cuts, the grazes, the blood and the bruises that were starting to bloom.

'Get me a bucket of warm water and some cloths,' she had said. The boys sprang into action. As Mrs Harlowe nursed her daughter behind a closed door, the boys looked at each other. Tony finally spoke. 'Let's go get them.'

He stormed out of the house, grabbed a thick plank from the woodpile and started heading back to town. Arthur followed his lead. They knew where to find each of the boys who had attacked Emily because they had grown up with them. Gone to school with them. Played on the same football team with them. They were the very ones whom Tony had joked were inferior. The ones who needed Arthur and Tony to win even a game of football. They found five of the eight boys that night and, adrenalin still throbbing, beat each one unconscious.

'The cops will be after us. We almost killed those bastards,' Tony had said. 'We should lay low for a while.'

'What will we do? We're only seventeen?'

'Almost eighteen. Remember that Tent Embassy I told you about. Was in the paper and they were talking about it yesterday at Tommy Boney's place.'

'Yeah.'

'Well, let's go there.'

'We've hardly been out of the town, except on football matches.'

'Then it's more likely no one will think to look for us there.'

They packed a few belongings and headed off.

They never spoke of the events of that night again.

Arthur thought nothing would lift his mood after what he had seen, that nothing could dispel his anxiety over Emily. Then, only days later, he had seen Beth Ann and fallen in love with her the first time he spoke to her. It filled him with hope but also with guilt.

Arthur loved Tony like a brother. He had seen what Tony had seen that night by the riverbank. He knew what it had taken out of him. So when Tony said, 'I'm really keen on her, Art, you know. Like no one before. Would you mind if I made a play for her?' how could he do anything but graciously bow out? Especially when Emily, whose handkerchief was tucked inside his pocket, was all battered and broken back home.

Arthur had known at the time he was giving up something precious. It was only as the years stretched and his feelings for Beth Ann still simmered that giving in to Tony's request that night became one of his greatest regrets.

When Tony left to follow Beth Ann to Sydney, Arthur went back to the mission. He arrived at night and knocked, late, on the door of Emily's house. The light was on. Tony's mother opened the door and, when she saw him, pulled him into her arms.

'How is Emily?' he asked. Mrs Harlowe started crying. Emily was a skeleton of her former self. She hardly spoke and rarely smiled. She seemed to barely recognise Arthur and would often stare at the wall.

He persevered. Every day he would sit with her. Would read her stories. Watch television. She stared blankly. Or worse, would sob.

One time, when he caught her crying, she whispered, 'I'm sorry.'

He fell on his knees before her. 'Emily, love, what do you have to be sorry for?'

'I lost the cross you gave me. It must have fallen off that night.'

'I'll get you another one,' he had said gently.

'It won't be the same,' she had whispered.

Three days later, she hung herself from a tree. No one said that they were surprised.

He stayed for the funeral, helped Mrs Harlowe with the arrangements. Tony came that day, arriving in the morning and hastily making his farewells the minute everyone began leaving the church. Arthur virtually lived with Mrs Harlowe for a while but eventually, he knew, he had to move away from Emily's shadow.

Unlike Tony, who never returned after the day of her funeral, he did come back from time to time. He came back with his fiancée, Sarah. He came back when both his girls were born. He would come back for the funerals of the old people whose stories he had heard.

And he built a happy enough life for himself. He loved his wife. He adored his daughters. He did the public service exam and worked in the Housing Department.

When his wife died of breast cancer at the age of thirty-eight, he devoted himself to being a father.

After all these years, he still held a place in his heart for Beth Ann. And, tucked in the top drawer of his side table, was the carefully folded handkerchief, his name spelled out in blue letters.

38

Tony's head was still thumping from the night before. He'd drunk too much at Patricia's and was feeling the worse for it now. He flicked through the transcripts Darren Brown had dropped off and tried to concentrate. The Legal Service was closed between Christmas and New Year but he thought that doing some work might take his mind off his troubles. It hadn't helped the way he had hoped.

His life had unravelled. Six months ago he had been smugly thinking about the dilemma of juggling a wife and a girlfriend. Now he was facing the new year alone. And as Patricia reminded him last night, no one would have any sympathy for him. He didn't know why he had gone to see her. His life had hit rock bottom. There were several women who would have happily given him some comfort but he chose the one who, he knew deep down inside, would tell him the truth.

He admired Patricia. Always had. He cringed when he thought of the clumsy pass he had made at her last night. Trust her to reject him so bluntly. He smiled at the thought. She was one of the few people in his life who was always honest with him – along with his mother, his daughter and Beth Ann. These four women were the mirrors of his true self.

When he had fled the mission, he had written those five steps for survival. One had said: 'Appeal to self-interest, never to mercy or gratitude'. The surest and best way to make your fortune, he had thought, was to let people see clearly that it's in their best interests to promote yours.

Always he tried to make people think they needed him. He knew Patricia never did. He had tried to make Beth Ann dependent on him. He had, through his own insecurity, distanced her from her family, made it difficult for her to see them. He had refused to allow her to take a paying job and had eventually agreed to one that was voluntary, and then only because he knew that, if she was in the prison all day, she could not contact him when he was up to no good.

He was more aware of his shortcomings than others would realise. That's why he invented his five steps for survival in the first place. So he could create a façade, so he could fool people.

And yet, Beth Ann had loved him and she was the one who knew him best. That day, that awful day, when she confronted him in the laundry, the evidence in her hand, he had fled. He couldn't face the hardness in her face, this look he had never seen before. He knew in his heart, by looking into her eyes, that she had turned cold against him. It was the second time in his life that he had run away.

He had thought at the time, justifying things to himself, that if he could legitimise his relationship with Rachel, it would make everything less shabby. When she had ended it with him, he'd been stunned. And hurt, he'd begrudgingly admitted to himself. But a deep part of him was relieved. He'd known as soon as he'd moved in with her it had been a mistake. But Beth Ann would give him no ground.

'I have packed your things. I would like to arrange to have them sent somewhere,' she had told him.

'I can come by and pick them up.'

'I'll be out between four and eight tomorrow. They'll be in the garage. I'll leave it unlocked.'

'Do you think they'll be safe there?'

'Don't know. Better come close to four then.'

'I'd like to see you.'

'I don't think that would be wise.'

Not rude but not welcoming. He had not expected her to beg. She was too dignified for that. It was one of the many things he loved about her. But her determined stoniness had given him no opportunity to talk about a reconciliation. He looked for every possible opening, any loose word. She gave him nothing and now he found himself heading towards a divorce that he didn't want.

His relationship with his daughter had improved but there was still a long way to go to properly repair it, to bring it back to what it had once been. He missed their talks and their rituals.

'How's my favourite daughter?' he would ask.

'I'm your only daughter,' she would reply.

'If I had a hundred daughters, you'd still be my favourite.'

It was silly but he had always loved it because it was *their* ritual, developed with affection and repeated over the years. Simone always smiled so brightly when they played the game. Lately she had refused to play along. He'd asked his lead question several times only to be rebuffed and it hurt too much to keep on trying.

Her angry early morning phone call had forced him to face what a coward he had been about Emily. He had used his rage at what had been done to her – and what he thought had been done to him – to make it impossible for him to stay. And he dreaded coming back to face her, his little sister who he could not protect. When she killed herself, he realised just how selfish, how irredeemably selfish he had been.

When Tony went home for the funeral he knew that he could never be in the town again, never be at the mission, never be in the house they grew up in, without seeing Emily and being confronted with how he had run away from her when she needed him the most. There was no place in that town where he would not have a memory of her, no place there where he would be able to forget her or his role in her death.

He had thought that the attention of others – the admiration of the Darren Browns and the Rachel Mileses of the world – would help him to forget his biggest failing, his biggest mistake, but now he realised that it didn't. It was a false sense of self he gleaned from their attention. It cultivated vanity, not self-esteem. Their adoration should be a pleasant compliment; it should not define him. He should enjoy it only if he could keep it in context, not get addicted to it.

Tony flicked through the transcripts one more time. Here, buried in his conversations with Darren Brown, was the thing that he really could be proud of. Here, in his work, was where he had been unselfish, where he had been courageous, where he had not run away.

George Orwell, still Tony's favourite writer, had said that the prime responsibility lay in being able to tell people what they do not wish to hear. Frederick Douglass, another of his heroes, had once said that those who expected truth or justice without struggle were like those who could imagine the sea without an image of the tempest. Noam Chomsky wrote that power quite probably knows the truth already and is mainly interested in distorting or suppressing it.

These great writers, great thinkers, great minds had given him courage and guidance in his work. When he was challenged by people asking, 'Who the hell do you think you are?' he would confidently reply 'Who the hell is asking?' When he was asked, 'How dare you intervene?' he would retort with 'How could I stand idly by?' To those who tried to embarrass him by the company he kept – communists, trade unionists, 'radical blacks' – he would point out that they were in dubious company themselves.

Yet, for all his achievements, for all he was proud of, his journey had been marked with mistakes and regrets.

He could not go forward – whichever way that might be – without going back. Hadn't that been what he had always told Simone? What he had been saying in his interviews with Darren? We need to understand our history before we can make sense of the future. It was one of his most used speeches.

His next step, he knew, was to finally return home.

Six Months Later . . .

39

'You seem to be having a lot of trouble sleeping lately,' Arthur sighed.

'Lucky you. Were you asleep?'

'In bed. Reading.'

'How can anyone sleep with all these police sirens?' Patricia asked as she watched the flashing lights and traffic below her window.

'You're the one who still wants to live in the middle of Redfern.'

Patricia ignored him. 'Remember how they used to come for us for no reason?'

'Sure do.'

'Now, with all these drug pushers moving in, the coppers are occasionally doing something useful.'

'It's a shame what these drugs are doing to young people. Back in our days there were plenty of problems with the grog and people would smoke that funny stuff but these hard drugs, they're something else.'

'Even though they sometimes clean up the pushers, I can't get over that deep hatred of coppers. I still remember how they would roughhouse us, that sound of bones cracking, the pain of being pulled by the hair or punched in the gut. And that's just what they did to us girls.'

'What's on your mind?'

'Our old friend Tony just left.'

'How's he holding up?'

'He was looking better than the last time I saw him.'

'He seems to be dropping by your place quite a bit lately. Don't tell me you are falling for his old charms,' Arthur joked.

'I'm not fooled by something so obvious. No. Once his life started falling apart, I guess he hoped that I would give him some support. You know, like a big sister.'

'You've always been there for us. All of us.'

'I know. I'm a black Mary Poppins.' There is a pause. 'Arthur,' Patricia says, 'I think I might have done something bad.'

'What do you mean?'

'Well, you know I think Tony brought a lot of his current circumstances upon himself, with his constant running around on Beth Ann. But I had a conversation with that young Rachel and I think I might have convinced her to leave Tony.'

'What do you mean?'

'I let her know that everyone was talking about her and Tony.'

'What did you do that for?'

'To tell you the truth, I didn't really think about it. I'm glad I spoke to her. She's so beautiful, full of promise. But I didn't do it for her. I could see the impact Tony's behaviour was having on Simone, but that wasn't the reason either. I did it for Beth Ann actually. I've always thought the world of her. At least, that was my motivation at the time, what I told myself. And you know, the more I sit back and see how things turned out, especially how miserable Tony is, I can't help but think that maybe I just should have kept my nose out of the whole business.'

'That's quite a confession.'

'I guess it is,' Patricia answered.

'What do you want me to say to make you feel less guilty?'

Patricia thought before answering. 'I don't know but I am open to suggestions.'

'Well, I can do better than that. I have a bit of a confession of my own to make. I've asked someone out, someone I gave up years back because I loved Tony so much. I loved them both all these years,. But now I've decided that — if it comes to it — I'll give Tony up instead.'

Patricia paused, looked out across the skyline. 'That is a very big decision. Are you ready to do this?'

'I can't let her go again, not if I have a chance.'

When Patricia finally hung up the phone, she felt wide awake. She thought about the night that Tony had come over after Rachel had thrown him out, thought about his fumbled attempt at seduction. She'd known by reading his face that he didn't mean it. He was drunk and blinded by his grief, scared that his life was spinning out of control, driven by desperation, not love. He was lost without Beth Ann and perhaps humiliated by Rachel's rejection. He needed reassurance.

Even though she still longed for him, Patricia was too proud to take him on those terms. Besides, she knew that he wouldn't stay. And there would be no being 'just friends' again. There was shallow comfort in the way that Tony still came to her for solace, but he had never again made any move, any suggestion. Each time he had been to see her since it was only as an old friend – talking over old times, new problems, friends, enemies, politics, philosophy.

After each of his visits, she'd console herself. It wasn't just the crumbs. This, she'd tell herself, was something.

40

Rachel clipped the plastic container shut. 'Lunch,' she announced proudly as she placed it into the backpack.

'Thanks,' Darren smiled back, his eyes locking with her gaze in the suspended time of fresh love.

'We'd better go or we'll miss the bus,' Rachel finally said.

She had not intended to go back to university but she found herself there as the new editor of the *Indigenous Law Journal* and Darren had re-enrolled to continue his law degree. She enjoyed being able to see him during the day between his classes and during her breaks.

Rachel had also been thinking about enrolling in a post-graduate degree ever since Patricia Tyndale had started suggesting it. While she always found it hard to say 'no' to Patricia about anything she also knew that it would be a good way for her to slowly build up her knowledge and expertise, to build a reputation for good work in her own right.

She knew her time with the Aboriginal Legal Service had been a disastrous first step in her career. She had enjoyed the work and was gaining confidence with her abilities but the relationship with Tony had over-shadowed everything else. If she hadn't had an ally in Patricia, she wondered how she ever could have summoned the courage to reinvent herself.

The few times she had seen Tony since they broke up were uncomfortable – he could not keep eye contact with her, would fidget, find an excuse to end the conversation. Working with him would have been impossible. She had made the right decision to move on.

Now she had Darren. He might not have Tony's experience or enjoyed the same status in the community but he had plenty of time to gain both. She enjoyed their conversations and shared interests, his stories about his grandmother and, perhaps most of all, his loving, tender way with her. Darren made her happy to just be herself.

Whenever Rachel thought of Carol Turner she would grin. Rachel had already left the Legal Service by the time Darren came back to pick up the transcripts Tony had been given to approve. As Darren told the story, when he walked through the door Carol had said, 'I think you came for these.' He nodded as she handed him an envelope. 'And this,' she'd added, scribbling Rachel's new email address on a scrap of paper.

Later in the day Darren will find the piece of paper slipped into his lunchbox.

*Their strange period establishing historical tradition –
8 letters.*

He will think about it during the afternoon, reverting to meditating on it during the lulls in his contracts lecture. He could never do cryptic crosswords before but there are tricks and, once you know them, they are easier to master. He is proud that he is learning to do them. It is just one more thing that Rachel has given him that he treasures.

Later that day he will smile as he writes at the bottom of her note – *heritage.*

41

'Hi Dad. What are you up to?'

'Just going through some notes for a meeting tomorrow. You know, catching up on my reading. This is a nice surprise.'

'I thought I better check up on my old pa. See how you are handling life in a shared house.'

'There are no all-night parties.' He seems to struggle to make a joke. 'Have you heard from your mother?'

'I spoke with her this morning.'

'How is she?'

'She's good. Enjoying her new jobs I think. Aren't you two talking?'

'She's asked me to leave her alone for a while.' He sounds forlorn, worn out.

'She probably thinks that is kinder for you both, you know.'

'Well, I miss her.'

'I know you do, Dad.'

I spoke to Mum earlier in the day. She is changing her name back to Beth Ann Gibson and told me she now better understood why Dad was always so focused on 'self-determination' and 'sovereignty'. 'There is nothing more liberating than taking control of your own life,' she announced. I have seen no signs of regret from her about the end of her marriage. The kindest thing I can do for my father is to change the subject.

'I just rang to say that I finished the book you sent me. I remembered when you read it to me the first time. I must have been about twelve. I didn't understand it then like I understood it this time.'

'He was always one of my favourites, George Orwell.'

'Even though it was about the Russian revolution, the message at its centre is kind of universal. The idea that a society's ideologies can be manipulated and twisted by those in positions of power is evident everywhere, even today.'

'Yes, it's the sad irony that the book encapsulates: that a utopian society is made impossible by the corrupting nature of the very power that is needed to make it. Orwell was a journalist, remember, and he knew the power of words. Especially of simplistic mantras, manipulative explanations and propaganda.'

'There was just one thing that puzzled me.'

'What was that?'

'The inscription on the inside cover. A list of five points.' I'd seen them as soon as I opened the book, scrawled in a version of Dad's writing:

1. Become someone new
2. Make sure you stay in the spotlight
3. Know who you are dealing with
4. Make people believe
5. Appeal to self-interest, never to mercy or gratitude

'It was a silly thing really. I wrote them down the night I left the mission with your Uncle Arthur and hitched my way to the Tent Embassy. Anyway, don't take any notice of them. They were a bit misguided, I think. But I wanted you to have the book. It was the only thing I took with me when I left home.'

'I admire the way you came from there and made something of your life, made something for me.'

'All you can do is try,' he says with resignation.

'Well, I better go,' I say.

'You know you're my favourite child, don't you?'

'I'm your only child.'

'But if I had a hundred, you'd still be my favourite.'

ACKNOWLEDGMENTS

The work of Gary Foley and John Maynard provided invaluable insights into the political background to the Tent Embassy and its lasting legacy. So did the many conversations I had with my father, talks that shaped my politics and my understanding of our history.

Extract on p. 49 from Kevin Gilbert, 'Because a White Man will Never Do It' reproduced with kind permission from his daughter Kerry Reed-Gilbert.

Christopher Hitchens's *Letters to a Young Contrarian*, Michael Dirda's *Book by Book* and Francine Prose's *Reading Like a Writer* were inspirations during the writing of this story.

Thank you to Madonna Duffy and Janet Hutchinson, Elyce Newton, Geoff Scott and my mother, Raema Behrendt.